EX'D OUT

EX'D OUT

A Melanie Bass Mystery

CHRISTINE FALCONE

First published by Level Best Books 2022

Author Photo Credit: Sara McIngvale Photography

First edition

ISBN: 978-1-68512-178-5

This book was professionally typeset on Reedsy.
Find out more at reedsy.com

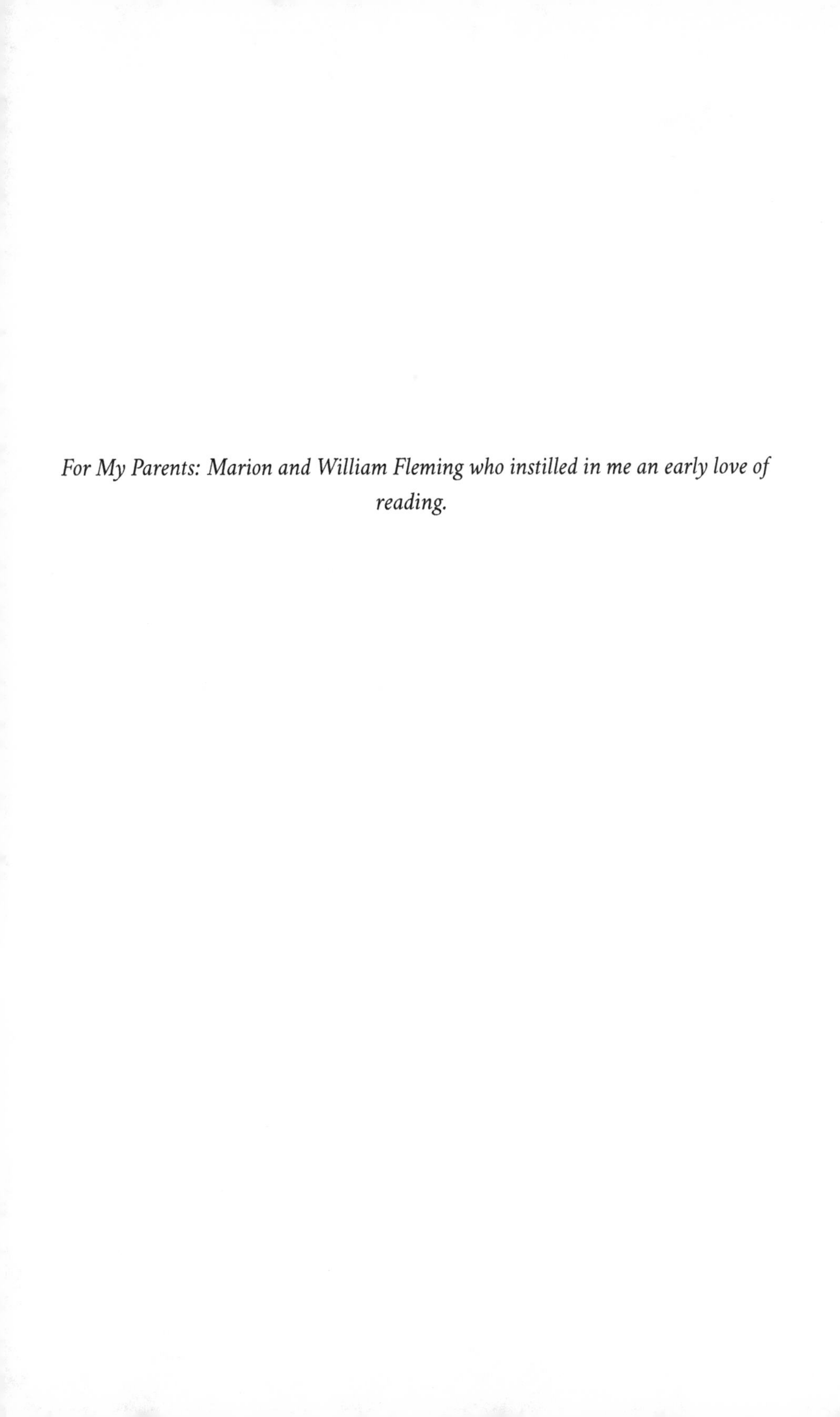

For My Parents: Marion and William Fleming who instilled in me an early love of reading.

Praise for Ex'd Out

"In her strong debut mystery, Christine Falcone introduces a loyal, clever, and dogged nursing sleuth. Melanie Bass is the kind of woman you'd want as your friend or neighbor—a heroine readers will root for."—Lucy Burdette, National Bestselling Author of *A Dish To Die For*

"Fans of crime fiction will welcome a savvy new sleuth, Melanie Bass, a nurse who knows death when she sees it."—Hallie Ephron, *New York Times* bestselling author of *Careful What You Wish For*

Chapter One

As soon as I pulled up next to Artie's red Mercedes in the rest stop parking lot, my blood pressure skyrocketed. He had parked under the shade of a towering maple, but the windows were rolled up, and Bruno was pawing frantically at the rear window. The glass was covered in dog slobber, and the little terrier was yelping. Artie was nowhere to be found. He had been named one of the "Top Dermatologists in Connecticut" in *Connecticut Magazine*, but my ex-husband sometimes lacked sense about the practical things in life. What kind of idiot leaves a dog closed in a car in the middle of July?

I yanked open the rear door, and Bruno jumped out, his leash still attached as if Artie was about to walk him. After I pet him and tried to calm him down, I reached into my car to grab the bowl and water I had stowed on the front seat. However, Bruno only lapped briefly from the water, then whined and strained on his leash. He led me toward the only other car in that area of the rest stop parking lot, a black Escalade parked several spaces away. He scratched at the passenger side door, and I said, "Off!" and pulled him away. I peered in the open passenger side window, ready to apologize to anyone who might be in the car.

A woman was slumped over the steering wheel, and a man in a light-colored suit had his face pressed into her lap. My first thought was that I'd interrupted something that would embarrass everyone involved if I didn't back away. Then I realized two things: what I'd first taken for shadows dappling the seat and the people inside was blood, and secondly, I recognized that linen-suit-clad form. I jerked the door open and pulled on Artie's arm to turn him over. He had two small bullet holes in his chest. I felt my insides collapse. The front of his suit was saturated with blood, as was the woman's lap where he had been lying. I felt under Artie's jaw for a pulse. His skin had begun to cool, and the only pulsing I felt was from the trembling of my own fingers. I went around to the other side of the car to check on the woman. When I opened the door, her arm fell from the steering wheel where it had been resting, and she started to slump slowly toward me. I reached out by reflex to stop her from tumbling out of her vehicle.

There was no need to feel for a pulse since the look of her head wound left no doubt she was dead, too. I suppressed a shudder and propped her back up in the position I had found her. I ran back to my own car to grab my cell phone off the front seat. I'd dropped Bruno's leash when I first opened the door of the Escalade, and I found him with his ears down and his tail between his legs, huddled against my left front tire.

I scooped Bruno up and crooned, "It's okay, it's okay" to him as I fumbled with the phone, even though we both knew it wasn't going to be okay. My hands shook as I punched in the numbers, but I managed to keep my voice calm as I reported finding Artie and the dead woman. At least I think I started out calm but must have ended up babbling because the 911 dispatcher kept repeating my words back to me as if for clarification.

"Are you sure the people are dead? I want you to feel—"

"I did. They're dead. I'm a nurse. I've seen dead before. CPR is not going to work now. Could you please send somebody right away?"

"What did you say your name was, miss?"

"Melanie Bass."

The tone of her voice was the same one I'd used countless times myself to calm hysterical patients and their families. "Okay, Miss Bass. Help is on the way. Just stay right where you are, okay? Promise me you won't leave the scene until the emergency vehicles arrive."

I suddenly realized what she was insinuating. "You don't think… I just found them; I had nothing to do with what happened."

"Stay on the line and stay where you are until help arrives, okay? I'm sure everything will be straightened out soon."

It seemed an eternity until I heard the faint cry of sirens approaching the rest stop. "They're here. I'm going to hang up." I wasn't sure who was trembling more now, Bruno or me. I held him tight against me as I waited for the ambulance and police cars to pull in. I'd sat with dying patients and their families and done postmortem care any number of times. But this – this was different from anything I'd experienced before. I couldn't even bear to look toward the black Escalade again.

As often as I'd wished Artie dead in the past, I'd never expected to find him in that state. He seemed so vulnerable lying there, and vulnerability was not a trait I'd ever associated with him in life. Artie had a nose for impending disaster and always acted to deflect it from himself. He never got a speeding ticket, no matter how much over the limit he drove. If patients were dissatisfied with their care, it was Artie who would call them from the practice and smooth it over. He called a divorce lawyer as soon as he found out I knew about his affair with his now wife, Tori. He'd said it was "Just to check the possible scenarios." That raised another important question, besides who shot him and why, which was what was he doing in the car with the dead woman? If past performance was an indicator, he was acting like a randy tom cat again, and maybe this time he'd upset someone enough to kill him. The woman bothered me, though. I realized I hadn't seen her at her best, but she looked to be maybe mid-forties and wearing a sleeveless denim shirt, jean shorts, and biker boots. I thought I knew Artie very well, and she just didn't look his "type." But why else was he with her? My thoughts were interrupted by what sounded like music. It seemed to be coming from the Escalade, but the sirens were becoming louder, and I couldn't be sure.

Bruno began to squirm in my arms, and I bent to put him down on the grassy area right in front of my car, his leash looped firmly around my wrist. An ambulance and two state police cars pulled into the rest stop.

I watched as the doors of the ambulance opened, and the paramedics rushed to the Escalade. Three of the police officers followed them, and a fourth, whose name tag read "Logan," approached me.

"Morning, miss. Are you all right? Have you sustained any injuries?"

I shook my head, unable to find my voice for a moment.

He took a pen and a small pad from the breast pocket of his uniform. "What is your name?"

"It's Melanie Bass."

"Could you spell that for me, please?" He wrote as I spelled it out. "Are you the one who called 911?"

"Yes, I was here to meet my ex-husband. He's the man in the Escalade." As we spoke, I glanced over toward where it was parked. A van with State of Connecticut Major Crimes had pulled up next to the Escalade, and another car pulled up next to where Officer Logan and I were talking. A woman got out of the car and strode up to us.

"Hello, Mitch." She shook his hand and nodded a greeting to me.

"Hi, Sunny. We just got started here. Basic info, we haven't gotten to what happened yet."

This new officer had on street clothes and had a badge on a lanyard around her neck that read "S. Cody."

The two officers spoke for a few minutes. I assumed Logan was giving her my name and my relationship to Artie. It looked like I would be speaking to Officer Cody now, as the other policeman moved away.

"Are you the one who found the victims?" She was at least six feet tall, towering over me by a good eight inches. Her dark brown hair was graying at the hairline and pulled back tightly into a ponytail. The parenthesis around her mouth, too severe to be mistaken for laugh lines, kept me from snapping back that if she looked, she'd notice there was no one else there but me. Actually though, as I glanced toward the fast-food restaurant across the parking lot, I could see that quite a crowd was forming as people strained to see what had caused such a large police presence.

"Yes, the man is my ex-husband, Dr. Arthur Kranpaneck." I hadn't expected my voice to catch as I said Artie's name. "I don't have any idea who the woman is. Was."

"And the car doors were open like that when you found them?"

I looked quickly toward where Officer Cody was pointing. I'd forgotten to close the doors in my haste to run and get my phone. "No. I opened the doors to check on Artie and the woman to see if I could help them."

The look on her face told me all I needed to know about how she felt about my answer. "You found your ex-husband dead, and you had the presence of mind to check him out rather than call 911 immediately for help?"

"Look, Officer—"

"Detective."

"Okay, Detective. I'm a nurse, and I just automatically responded by assessing what condition he, and the woman, were in. Just in case there was something I could do before calling for help. I didn't know they were dead until I checked."

"What did you touch besides the car doors? Did you touch both of the deceased to, as you stated, check on them?" She took out a small notebook and began to write in it.

I nodded. "Yes. But then I ran back to my car to call 911. I don't think I touched anything else in the car."

"Okay, so back up to why you came here, and what you saw when you got here. Why don't we start with what time you arrived?"

I took a deep breath and re-capped for Detective Cody what I had found when I arrived to meet Artie.

"And you were meeting your ex-husband at this rest stop because….?'

"We were supposed to exchange custody of our dog." I motioned to Bruno, who seemed to be watching both the detective and me expectantly. "After our divorce, we agreed to share possession of him, so he wouldn't be confused by losing either of us."

Detective Cody lifted one eyebrow, but before she could say anything else, one of the other officers approached her. "Sunny, Escalade contains one female occupant and one male, both deceased. No IDs. Wallets and purse are gone. No registration in the Escalade, but the Mercedes is registered to Arthur J. Krapaneck." He held up Artie's cell phone, now encased in a plastic bag. "I found this in the Escalade, wedged between the passenger seat and the center console. It shows one missed call. Time of the call was fifteen minutes ago."

What I had heard as music a few minutes ago must have been the ringtone from Artie's phone.

Detective Cody took the phone and held it out to me. "Is this your ex-husband's phone?"

"Yes, it is."

"Do you recognize the number?"

Even through the plastic bag it was encased in, I could see the "missed call" and the number still displayed on the screen. "That's his office. High Life Dermatology Associates. He did mention he had an early appointment today."

Detective Cody nodded and handed the phone back to the uniformed officer.

"Did he mention who the appointment was with?" She jotted more notes in her little notebook.

"No. We only spoke about meeting here and me picking up Bruno."

She glanced down at what she had on her pad. "You said your name is Bass, not Krapaneck like the victim."

"After the divorce I changed my name back to Bass."

She scratched out something she had written. "Ms. Bass, then. You were meeting your ex-husband to pick up your dog, right? So why was the woman in the Escalade here?"

"I told you I don't know. Artie remarried a year and a half ago. That's not his wife, Tori, and it's not my business who Artie meets any longer. My only interest was in getting Bruno." It sounded a little cold, but in fact, it irked me a little that I had no idea why Artie and this woman were together. "Do you think it could have been a robbery?" That was a scary thought. If so, what if I'd gotten here earlier? Would that have prevented the crime, or would I have been another victim?

"Robbery is certainly one possibility." Detective Cody looked toward the Escalade, where a horde of technicians was taking pictures and busily going through the SUV. "We'll see. I wouldn't want to jump to any conclusions just yet."

I had followed her glance toward the Escalade, and realized I knew one of the investigators from the Medical Examiner's office. His name was Paul Ascue, and I'd known him since college. He'd dated a member of my group of friends. She was totally smitten with him, but we always referred to him as P.A. I think he assumed it was an affectionate nickname we had given him. Actually, it stood for Pompous Ass. I prayed he wouldn't notice me.

Detective Cody followed my gaze, and what looked like a hint of a smile started to form on her face, then was gone just as suddenly. "Did Dr. Krapaneck have any enemies that you knew of?"

"Artie had a way of making you either love him or hate him." As soon as I said it, I realized that I may have sounded a tad harsh.

Once again, she scratched a few things in her notebook, then pinned me with her arctic grey eyes. "Which category were you in?"

A wave of apprehension washed over me. I quickly glanced down to be sure I didn't have blood on me from when I'd touched Artie and the woman. Thankfully, I did not. I was pretty sure detective Cody had already checked to make sure I didn't also. "Neither. I was angry at Artie when we first split, but now we are civil to each other. Were civil." Bruno whined.

"So, can you think of anyone who does hate Dr. Krapaneck?"

I could think of one or two, depending on what relationship it turned out he had with the dead woman, but I would think that would be obvious to the police. "Maybe I should rephrase what I said about people either loving or hating Artie. It's more that some people thought he was an arrogant jerk. I can't think of anyone who would want to murder him, though. Unless the dead woman was married, or ...no. Tori wouldn't kill Artie." The idea was laughable.

Detective Cody paused as if to make a note in her notebook. "Who's Tori, again?"

"Tori is his wife. She would strip Artie naked in a divorce settlement, but not shoot him." That reminded me that Tori probably didn't know what happened yet, and I felt a twinge of pity for her. "Someone needs to notify her. Let her know what's happened to Artie."

"One of my colleagues will speak to Mrs. Krapaneck." The detective slipped her notebook into a pocket. "I think that's all for now, Ms. Bass, but you will need to be available should we have any more questions. Please give your contact information to officer Draken." She motioned to the policeman who had brought her the phone.

"Of course." I gave Officer Draken my name, address, and phone numbers, then I sat down on the bench of one of the picnic tables near my car. I suddenly felt all the adrenaline drain from my body, making my knees begin to shake and my hands tingle.

Officer Draken gave me a worried look, "Are you okay, miss?"

What I was feeling must have shown plainly on my face. I nodded. "I'm all right. I just need to sit for a moment." I gave him what I realized was a weak smile.

I made it a point not to look over toward what was going on at the Escalade again. As my nerves were recovering from the jolt of seeing Artie and his companion dead, my mind began to race. I had a lot of questions of my own. The element of time, for one thing. I was supposed to meet Artie at 7:30, and he'd obviously arrived earlier than planned. Artie was always late. So, he must have planned to meet the dead woman before me, and that didn't sound like something you'd do if you were arranging a tryst. Bruno got up to pace in front of me, so I walked him on the grassy area around the picnic area. As Bruno sniffed around, I ran all the possibilities over in my mind trying to come up with a possible explanation. A familiar voice stopped me.

"Melanie!"

It was P.A.

"Artie, dead. My God! Well, I guess with his penchant for screwing anything in a skirt, it was inevitable that he'd anger the wrong person one day." He curled his lip in distaste, then must have remembered that I'd once been married to the guy. "Oh, sorry. I didn't mean to be disrespectful, but he did have a reputation, you know."

I decided to ignore his tactlessness in the interest of pumping him for information. "Is that what you think happened? That they were both shot by a jealous lover?"

"Well, I don't know. That is the first thought that came to my mind, however."

I didn't feel the need to share with him that that was my first thought also. "Could you tell exactly what happened?"

"They both suffered fatal gunshot wounds, of course."

Stupid Ass was more like it. "I realize that. I meant do you know if the police found anything that might lead them to whoever did this? Maybe you overheard them speculating or something?"

He pulled up to his full five feet seven inches. "You know that if I did, I couldn't share the information with you."

It was weak, but I figured I had nothing to lose in asking. "Not even as a fellow medical professional?" I never got to hear his reply.

"Hey, Paul, come over here a minute, would ya?" One of the officers summoned him back toward the crime scene.

"Take care of yourself, Mel." He patted my arm stiffly.

As he strutted away, Bruno barked and pulled at his leash.

I glanced back toward where I'd found the bodies. The paramedics had placed both Artie and the mystery woman in body bags and were loading them into the back of the ambulance. Detective Cody came back over to me as I turned away from the scene.

"Ms. Bass, are you going to be all right to drive yourself home?"

"Yes." I didn't know whether she was genuinely concerned or if it was a subtle message to "Move along, now."

"What about his partners? Should I call them?"

"We'll take care of that." She turned and went back to speak to the other officers gathered around the dead woman's car.

I lifted Bruno into the front seat of my car, his crate in the back forgotten. I needed to feel the warmth from his body as he snuggled against my side. I'd told Detective Cody I was fine to drive home, but I realized I had that hollowed-out feeling that follows a shocking event. I climbed behind the wheel and pretended to be looking for something in my purse as I tried to calm myself. When I looked up Det. Cody was looking back at me. I gave her a tentative wave and started toward home.

Chapter Two

Bruno started out by my side, but quickly ended up with his head in my lap. He looked up at me occasionally as if to say, "Are you okay, Mom?" I wasn't. I had to keep reminding myself to relax my arms and take a deep breath as I drove us home. By the time I pulled into our little crushed shell driveway, Bruno was sitting up on my lap as if he thought he should take the wheel.

I had been resentful at first when Artie built a huge house for Tori after our divorce. I had planned our dream house shortly after Artie and I had married, a house that we endlessly discussed, but never got around to building. However now I'd come to think that maybe I'd gotten the better side of the deal after all. While nothing like the mansion I'd imagined, I had a cozy cottage opposite a salt marsh with a fantastic view of the sunset. I took a moment to look around and ground myself in the moment before I let Bruno out of the car and headed into the house.

After I put out fresh water for the dog and made myself a cup of hot tea, I called Judy Pelzer, my supervisor. I was working at Coretrack, a visiting nurse agency. Even though it was technically my day off, I had agreed to see one patient that afternoon as a favor to her.

"Could you see if Debbie or Sherry will check on Mr. Duggan today? I've had a rough morning, and I don't think I could handle him right now."

"What happened? Are you okay?" Judy asked.

"It's Artie." I was horrified as I realized my answer had come out as a sob. "He's dead. Murdered. And there was some dead woman with him. I found them."

CHAPTER TWO

"Oh my God! Where?"

I told her what had happened at the rest stop, the details pouring out of me like wine at an Italian wedding.

"That's horrible. Do they know who did it?" she asked.

"No. They think it could have been a robbery."

"I can't blame you for being so shook up. I'm so sorry. I know you and Artie were divorced, but still…." I could hear her rustling papers as if she was looking for something. "Let me see— well, we can count Debbie out. After her last visit to Mr. Duggan she swore she'd quit before she went to see that old coot again. Her words, not mine. Sherry's away on a cruise. We're pretty booked up all day. You saw him at the end of last week. Do you think he can wait until tomorrow or the next day to be seen?"

I wanted to say yes. I wanted to just take the afternoon to sort out how I felt, try to wrap my mind around finding Artie and the mystery woman like that. "No. The guy's a mess. He hasn't been checking his blood sugar as often as he needs to, and he won't let the Home Health Aide in to do his foot care. There was a blanched area on his left foot I'm a bit worried about." I sighed. "I'll just go and make sure he's all right, see what kind of food he has in the house, and make him check his blood sugar while I'm there."

"No, you will not. I'll see if we can reschedule someone else and have one of the other nurses stop by Mr. Duggan's." Judy's voice was firm, and it was tempting to let her adjust the schedule, but I decided it would be better if I went to see him after all.

"Thanks anyway, Judy, but it might help if I just didn't think about what happened this morning. This will be something else to focus on." I was starting to feel less at odds and ends, more in control of my emotions.

There was a brief pause on Judy's end. "If you're sure that's what you want to do. But I owe you big time, sweetie."

Charlie Duggan lived alone in a three-bedroom house on one acre of land in Guilford. His house stood out in a neighborhood where homes twice the size of his were built on land half the size of his property. When he was in a good mood, we had interesting conversations about his former profession in private security and his theories about how this country was "going to hell in a handbasket." When he was not in a good mood, things didn't go as well.

I knocked loudly on his front door since Mr. Duggan still liked to monitor the safety of the area, and often had his police scanner on, and loud squeals and static had interrupted our visits in the past. Also, he was slightly hard of hearing.

"Jaysus! I can hear you; you don't have to break the door down. Who's there?"

"It's Melanie Bass from Coretrack Visiting Nurses, Mr. Duggan."

"Why are you here today? Is this the day you're supposed to come?" He continued to talk to me through the closed door.

"Yes. Remember I saw you Friday, and I said I would be back today to check on you? Please open the door so we can talk inside."

"What're you planning on doing today?" The door remained closed.

"I just want to help you check your sugar, see that you are all right."

"Well, I feel fine today. Come back another day, no sense wasting my time and the insurance company's money, thieving bastards though they are."

I tried to keep the irritation out of my voice. "Mr. Duggan, I'm not leaving until you let me in. You promised me on Friday you would let me in without an argument when I came today."

"I changed my mind."

I could feel the blood begin to pound in my temples. "You can't 'change your mind'! This is serious. You could die. Do you want to die?" I was immediately appalled at my loss of control. I always prided myself on my ability to deal with the most difficult of patients. I shouldn't have let what happened that morning affect how I dealt with Mr. Duggan.

There was silence on the other side of the door. Somehow, I didn't think my outburst bothered him too much.

"Charlie? Do you want me to call the police, tell them I need them to break down the door because I'm worried my patient is in a diabetic coma?"

The door opened before I finished speaking. "Damn know it all. You're bluffing, but I don't got all day to stand here and argue."

The smell of decaying flesh was obvious as soon as he opened the door, as well as his inability to bear weight on his left foot. He had no slipper on the foot and was using a gnarled old walking stick to lean on.

Charlie limped over to a sofa cluttered with blankets and paperback books and plunked himself down. He shoved an empty coffee cup and the case that held his glucometer supplies out of the way on the coffee table so I could put my bag down. “If you got to do this, hurry up, would ya? I’m about to find out who was killing all them girls.” He motioned to an open book on the coffee table.

We were interrupted just then by a loud run of static from his police scanner followed by a series of numbers which meant nothing to me. I walked over and turned the volume down, then kneeled in front of him to examine his foot.

I was aghast at what it looked like when I unwrapped the makeshift dressing around it. “Charlie, you know I have to call Dr. Moore right away about this.”

“It’s fine. Just put some of that goop you always use on it.”

I shook my head. “No, you need this treated right away.” I straightened up and took out my cell phone, “I’m calling the doctor and then an ambulance.”

“Don’t call no ambulance! I’ll sic the dog on’um if they come.”

I knew his dog well; he was a nearly toothless Pomeranian who seemed to always be curled up asleep in Charlie’s armchair. “No, you won’t. If something happened to you who would take care of him?” The dog stretched out and emitted a creaking yawn as I gently stroked his head.

Charlie looked off into space as if he saw doom on the horizon. “Here, give me your phone. I got to call my grandson to take Rex for a couple of days, I guess.” He glared at me, his eyes magnified by the thick lenses of his reading glasses.

As we waited for the ambulance, I redressed his foot and checked his blood sugar, which wasn’t as high as I feared. However, it turned out he hadn’t taken his insulin since the previous night and only ate pretzels for breakfast.

“Charlie, you have to take better care of yourself. I know your daughter checks on you. Have you been telling her the truth about how you’re doing?”

He wouldn’t meet my gaze. “Mostly.”

By the time I got Charlie Duggan packed off to the hospital, I was totally drained. He'd gotten up enough steam to give the paramedics a rough time, even if the dog hadn't. He tried to bite them himself when they called him "Pops."

It was midafternoon when I finished my charting on Mr. Duggan. I had planned to stop at the store and get something for dinner on my way home, but I had no appetite—for food or more human contact. The day was cooling down nicely. In another hour or so, the crowds at Hammonassett Beach State Park would thin, and a long walk with Bruno along the bike path sounded good. Running and walking are the ways I use to work off stress.

One of the things Artie and I had disagreed about when we were discussing building our ideal house was where to build it. I wanted a house on the ocean, or as close to it as possible. I had grown up in a Connecticut Shoreline town, not on the water in a house like we could now afford, but it had always been my dream to live there. He argued that we would be in danger of flood if there was a hurricane or severe storm, and what about the garden and grape arbor I wanted? Wouldn't the sea air be bad for that? He protested that he was only thinking of me. He didn't want me to realize when it was too late that his choice of location would be better suited to the home I wanted. In spite of my reassurances that even if we built a house that was not directly on the shoreline, severe storms could still cause damage, and things actually do grow and thrive near the beach. He would not be moved. Finally, he argued, he was raised far from the ocean, and he was sure the sound of crashing waves would keep him awake at night.

Hammonassett Beach State Park is the largest park in Connecticut, with a beach that stretches for two miles. It has picnic pavilions, a nature center, and camping grounds. In summer, the beach is usually packed until the park closes at sunset, but dogs are forbidden on the beach itself. Instead, I headed for the bike and walking path that snakes along the dunes and beach roses that separate it from the sandy beach itself. There were few other people walking or riding their bikes, fewer even than I'd expected. Or maybe I was just noticing my surroundings more because of what happened with Artie. Even though I knew the most likely scenario was that once again Artie was cheating, this time on Tori, there was still the possibility that he and the woman were the victims of a robbery. The thought that Artie was being unfaithful to Tori made me feel sad, though I couldn't say why. She had been the other woman when I was married to Artie. She was a pharmaceutical rep who met him on one of her rounds and just decided she wanted him, married or not. I had no love for her, but I thought that Artie was really trying to make their marriage work. But then, I'd thought he was trying to make our marriage work, so what did I know?

I picked up Bruno and started to jog. Just because I needed to outrun my feelings was no reason to stress his little body. The dog looked up at me like I was out of my mind but tolerated being cradled as I plugged along until I was so sweaty and out of breath a shower and a tall glass of iced tea were all I could think about.

When I got into the house, the light on the answering machine was blinking. The voice was hesitant at first. "Melanie, this is Tori. Krapaneck." There was a long drawn in breath followed by a sob. "Could you call me when you get this message?"

Tori had called me only a total of four or five times in the two years since Artie and I had been divorced. None of the times had ended up as a pleasant conversation. I decided to wait until the next day to call her back. I was exhausted by the strong emotion of the day and not sure how I would be able to deal with whatever Tori wanted. I immediately felt ashamed, however. She was the widow, and I should show more compassion for what she was going through. Also, I realized, maybe the police had given her more info than they'd shared with me. I drew in a breath of my own, then picked up the phone.

The voice of the woman who answered my call resembled Tori's but was deeper.

"Victoria isn't available right now. I'm her sister. She's resting and can't be disturbed. I'll see that she gets the message that you returned her call."

"Thanks. Oh, and I was wondering if arrangements have been made yet for services for Artie. If she needs help—"

"We are waiting for the authorities to release Arthur's remains. However,

Victoria and I have everything under control."

I wondered if her usual tone of voice was frosty, or if she recognized me as the ex. In any case, I felt as if a small burden had been lifted. I was satisfied that I had tried to do the right thing by returning Tori's call. I flicked on the TV but had missed all the local newscasts. I planned to stay up for the late news to see if there was any more information but gave up when I could no longer hold my head up. I drifted into sleep, only to have a dream that Artie was standing in front of me. He was angry that his favorite suit was stained by blood, and he kept wiping my mouth with a wet cloth as I struggled to get away. I came fully awake to Bruno licking my chin. I settled him under my arm and went back to a restless sleep.

Chapter Three

I woke up feeling achy and exhausted the next morning, wondering for a moment if Artie's death had been only one of my strange dreams of the night before. I threw on a T-shirt and a pair of jersey running shorts and grabbed Bruno's leash. I tried not to think of what had happened, but the more I tried to put it out of my mind, the more bits and pieces of what I'd seen came back. And some of these pieces didn't fit with the robbery theory. I remembered the inside of the vehicle as empty except for Artie and the woman. The police had said their valuables were missing, and it was true that I'd only had a brief look and was concentrating on attempting to help Artie and the woman, but there was no debris. No empty coffee cups, no papers flung around or an open glove box like someone was looking for valuables. And why shoot them, not just rob them? The passenger side window was down, as if Artie had been talking to someone he knew, or at least didn't feel was a threat to him. Detective Cody hadn't seemed particularly convinced it had been a robbery, and I was beginning to question my knee jerk theory that Artie was cheating on Tori. That left the question she had posed to me the previous day: who hated Artie enough to kill him?

Another thought occurred to me. Wouldn't it be ironic if it was the woman who was the intended victim? I had to smile just a bit at that thought: self-important Artie Krapaneck merely a bit player in the final drama of his life.

I figured it was too early to call the police station to see if I could get an update on the case, or if they had found out who the mystery woman was. The sun was coming up in streaks of orange and pink, and a soft breeze had started to clear the mist from the marsh across the road from my house. I stopped to watch an egret lift off from among the reeds. Bruno trotted along as if nothing had changed in dogdom, but even though I'd been divorced from Artie for over two years, I felt a big piece of my life had shifted. It felt like an argument unfinished. I jogged more than my usual mile and a half, making myself concentrate on my breathing and the feel of the road under my feet, slowing only as I felt Bruno tire a bit. My mind cleared, at least for the time being.

By the time we got back from our run, the newspaper was at the bottom of my driveway. There was a file photo of Artie, one of his better ones, just below the crease on the front page. The headline read: "Prominent Local Physician Killed." The article named some of Artie's many professional awards and went on to say that the police were investigating robbery as a motive for the killing. The article mentioned there had been a woman killed also, her identity was being withheld pending notification of her next of kin. There was nothing there I didn't already know.

I threw the paper on the kitchen table and showered and dressed for work.

I waited until early afternoon to call the police station, assuming that by then they might have more information. The person who answered the phone was brusque. "Cody's not in right now. Do you want to leave a message?"

"Yes, this is Melanie Bass. I was wondering if she could return my call. It's about Artie Krapaneck, the man who was found murdered yesterday."

"Yeah, I remember. You have something you forgot to tell her?"

"No, I was just wondering if there was any more information on how or why she thinks it happened."

"You watch the news? What she's going to tell you is on there."

"It's just that I knew Artie better than anybody…or at least at one time I did, and something isn't right about what you are saying happened."

"How much detective work you doing these days? Unless you're with the freakin' CSI I think you better leave the crime reconstruction to us. Or maybe you have some intimate knowledge of exactly what *did* happen yesterday?"

"No. I'm sorry. I didn't mean to imply you didn't know what you were doing. Could you ask Detective Cody to call me, though? I gave her my phone numbers yesterday."

"I'll give her your message."

I told myself I had done nothing wrong by trying to find out more about Artie's death, but the desk officer's attitude made me feel slightly guilty.

After seeing my afternoon patients, I decided to stop in and check on Mr. Duggan. There had been no call from Detective Cody, and I figured there probably wasn't going to be one. I wondered if Prince Charming at the desk had even given her my message.

A call to patient information got me the floor to which Mr. Duggan had been admitted. I called the Surgical ICU, where he had been sent post-op, and spoke to his nurse. I explained I had been following him through Coretrack Homecare and hoped to get an update on his condition. It turned out he had been about three bacteria short of a generalized septicemia upon admission. He'd been the first case that morning for a below-the-knee amputation of his left leg.

It had been three years since I'd stopped working there, but each time I came to visit a patient at University Hospital, I got the same "coming home" feeling. The building, many of the faces, the feel of the hospital itself were familiar and comfortable. I'd left after an incident with an attending physician who I felt was not always acting in the best interests of his patients. I didn't like how my complaint was handled by the administration. Also, Artie had recently started in practice with three other dermatologists, and I thought it would be good for our marriage to work together.

I took the elevator to the third floor where the Surgical Intensive Care unit was located. As I approached the security doors where I would need to be buzzed in, I heard a familiar voice behind me.

"Melanie? I thought that was you. What are you doing here?"

Kayla Rockland and I had gone to nursing school together and occasionally met for lunch at the hospital when I'd worked there. We exchanged a quick hug. "I'm with Coretrack Homecare now. One of my patients was admitted yesterday afternoon, and I came to see how he was doing."

She slid her badge through the slot outside the unit, and the doors swung open. I followed her in. "Who's your patient?"

"Charles Duggan. A diabetic with a b.k. amputation done this morning."

She snorted, "He's not my patient, but I took the report on him from the Post Anesthesia Recovery Unit. From what I hear, he's hell on wheels."

As we approached the front desk in the Surgical ICU., she put her hand on my back and pulled me aside. "I heard what happened to Artie. It's terrible. I know he was a jerk to you, but still…."

"It's kind of weird, but all the resentment and anger I felt toward him seems petty now," I said.

"Speaking of resentment and anger—have you heard that that cretin, Ben Haupt, left for 'professional' reasons?" She smiled.

I cringed at the mention of his name. Ben Haupt had been part of the reason I left University Hospital. "Yeah, I did hear something about that."

"He tried to intimidate a new grad this time, he threw a water pitcher at her when she questioned his order on a patient. He didn't realize the patient in that room was just shuffling out of the bathroom and saw the whole thing."

"I'm surprised they let him have the dignity of resigning." Memories of my own resignation after the administration reprimanded him but did not suspend him for a similar incident in which I was involved flashed through my mind.

"Well, that's how *he*'s putting it. In fact, he was told to update the resident-on-call about his patients, and security very quietly escorted him off the floor. He'll doubtless appeal before the review board, but hopefully, they will see the pattern in his behavior this time."

"How is the nurse he tried to bully?"

"Fine. She let him know she wasn't having it. A lot like you. I was surprised to hear you'd left after he reported you for insubordination." Kayla said.

"It was a bad time in my life. Artie and I had been arguing a lot, and I was starting to have suspicions that he was cheating on me. Then that arrogant fool Haupt insisted I take a verbal order that I knew was wrong. Silly me, I thought Artie would hire me to help in his practice. He said he thought it would be 'too distracting working with his wife'. It took me a while to figure out the real reason was he was banging the pharmaceutical rep in his office."

"I heard that Artie brought up the incident that occurred between you and Haupt at the board meeting where they decided to fire the creep. I heard he was quite adamant that Ben be terminated this time and was able to convince the rest of the board."

I was touched to hear he had finally decided to stand up for the nursing staff, but I couldn't help but feel a bit of resentment also. "Well, good for him. I only wish he'd been that supportive when it happened. to me."

"Anyway, I'm sorry about Artie." She hugged me again. "So, they're saying it was a robbery? What do you think?"

"I don't know. I guess that's the most likely explanation." After my conversation with the officer who had been at the desk that morning, I decided to keep my suspicions to myself for the time being. I checked my watch; it was getting late, and I had to get home to let Bruno out. "Which cubicle did you say Mr. Duggan was in?"

"Four. Let me know what the funeral arrangements are for Artie."

Charlie had better color than the last time I had seen him, despite the multitude of IV lines and the catheter he sprouted. His nurse, Cindy, was taking his vital signs.

I explained who I was and that I had come to check on him.

"Mr. Duggan? Hey Charlie! Miss Bass is here to see you." She yelled about three inches from his ear.

He smacked his lips twice as he tried to find his voice, then croaked, "Hear, dammit." His eyes briefly cracked open to slits, and he whispered, "You. Here." Then he seemed to drift off again, no doubt courtesy of some well-deserved pain medication.

"He's doing well." Cindy said. "His sugars have stabilized, and his vitals are rock stable. If this keeps up, he'll probably be transferred out to the surgical floor tonight or tomorrow."

"Great," I said and put a small bag with two paperback mysteries on his bedside cart. "Could you make sure these go with him when he gets transferred? I know he'll want something to read when he is more alert." I hoped he'd like my choices: a golf mystery and one about a detective in Savannah, Georgia. I knew that he'd let me know loud and clear what he thought of them the next time I saw him.

I could hear the phone ringing as I unlocked my back door. Bruno's licking of my hands and dancing around my ankles slowed me down, and Tori's voice was just starting to be picked up by the machine again when I got to the phone.

"Hello."

"Melanie? Whyn't you answer your cell phone?"

I checked and saw I had one missed call. "Sorry, it was on vibrate."

"I'm afraid I was un'vailable when you called back last night. It's been—difficult." Her voice sounded a bit slurred at first, but then she cleared her throat, and it was her usual throaty, in-command pitch I remembered.

"Of course. I understand. Have you been able to make funeral arrangements yet?"

"The coroner's office said they would release his—him—tomorrow. There won't be any calling hours. That would just be too hard for me, so family only viewing Friday night. However, you're welcome to attend the funeral Saturday at St. Margaret's."

Her comments took me by surprise. I hadn't thought I'd need permission to attend Artie's funeral, for goodness sake, but I bit my tongue. It didn't seem appropriate to be rude to her so soon after her husband had been murdered, even if he'd been my husband first.

"All right. Is there anything I can help you with?"

"Zeta is here to help."

Zeta must be the sister. She paused for a few seconds while I wondered what the purpose of her call really was. "Did you ever see Artie meeting anyone else while you were picking up or dropping off the dog?"

Ah, so it was finally occurring to her to wonder what Artie was doing with the woman. "No, we spoke very little and only about what was necessary regarding Bruno. I really have no idea who the woman was or why he was in her car. The police already asked, and I told them all I know."

"The police asked me, too. He's had an awful lot of early morning meetings lately; he said they were with you. And lately I've had the feeling....and sometimes he looked at me like....never mind. I just hope you won't let the past cause you to get back at me by withholding information. If you knew Artie was cheating on me, I hope you would have let me know."

Apparently not too early for the widow to be a bit bitchy. "Now, wait a moment—"

"No need to climb on your high horse. Sorry to bother you."

She hung up before I could respond again. As I put the phone down, I couldn't help but wonder what *that* was about.

The comment about holding a grudge *did* strike a chord with me because, frankly, I did. Sort of. I hadn't wanted Artie back, but it still stung that Tori had blatantly decided she wanted him, wife or no wife, and set out to get him. As a pharmaceutical representative, she met him on one of her sales calls to High Life Dermatology Associates. She bagged both the High Life account for Rafkin Pharmaceuticals and Artie for herself. Of course, she didn't work for Rafkin any longer. She had resigned shortly after she married Artie. Most importantly, however, I held it against her that she didn't like Bruno. She tolerated him, at least according to Artie, but animals just weren't her "thing."

Still, I wouldn't have lied or covered up for Artie. Especially not if knowing the truth would have made Tori's life miserable. It also annoyed me that Artie had used me as an excuse to cover up whatever he was really doing. I'd only seen him briefly of late, just to pick up or drop off Bruno. And come to think of it, he had seemed a little tense, almost as if he wanted to tell me something, then thought better of it.

Chapter Four

The church was packed. I recognized a lot of the staff from University Hospital, and of course, his partners and office staff with their spouses and significant others. Many of the rest of those present, I assumed, were former patients, but Artie had also been active in the community and had scores of acquaintances and social contacts. Artie's parents were both deceased, and he was estranged from his only brother, Carter. I knew they had had an argument after their parents' deaths, but it seemed to me that the phrase "over my dead body" should have been forgotten here, and the man should attend his own brother's funeral. I had never met Carter, so searched the crowd for someone who looked as if he could be related to Artie, but no one seemed to fit the bill.

The first row was empty, reserved for the current Mrs. Kranpaneck, I supposed. I thought that as Artie's ex-wife, I could have sat in the second pew, sort of immediate family once removed, but instead, I sat a couple of rows back with one of Artie's partners, Bobby Wang, and his wife, Susan. We had often socialized with the Wangs during our marriage, and as a matter of fact, Bobby had served as Best Man at our wedding in this very church. After the divorce, I found out that Bobby tried, obviously to no avail, to convince Artie what an ass he was being to cheat on me with Tori. Bobby put his arm around me, and Susan reached across him to squeeze my hand after I sat down.

Organ music began to play, signaling the imminent entrance of the casket and funeral entourage. A very blonde, very tanned woman who looked to be in her forties entered and quickly slipped into the second row, two rows ahead of me. Susan leaned past Bobby and mouthed to me, "Who's that?"

I shrugged. By the look of her skin, probably another patient, or at least she should have been. I gave her credit for having a lot of nerve to sit where close relations usually sat. My thought about what was and what was not proper placement of mourners was interrupted by a muffled sob coming from a pew at the rear of the church. I turned to see Renata Wells, the practice's office manager, covering her mouth with a handkerchief. Malcolm Devlin, another partner in the practice, was by her side and patting her back in a consolatory way.

There was a momentary pause in the music, then it swelled as the doors at the rear of the church opened, and Artie made his last earthly entrance. Tori followed the casket as it was rolled down the aisle by the pallbearers. With her was another slightly older woman whom I thought must be her sister as they bore a strong resemblance to each other. The woman had her right arm through Tori's left, as Tori used her right hand to dab at her eyes with a pink tissue. Behind them was a tall dark-haired man, who ducked into a back pew, obviously embarrassed at his late arrival.

That unreal feeling came over me again. It was hard to believe Artie was gone. I felt tears start to well up, but as Tori passed me, she met my eyes briefly, and I remembered her suspicions of a couple of nights ago. Artie had been using meeting me as an excuse for whatever he was up to, and this audacity was so typical of him it dried my tears.

The service was beautiful. I had to admit Tori and her sister had done a great job choosing the hymns and readings. I had forgotten what a wonderful person most people thought Artie was until I heard it recounted in the three eulogies offered. Caring physician, patron of the Arts, animal lover. That last made me exclaim "ha!" but I covered it, pretending it was a sob. Artie had not wanted a dog, and while he did come to love Bruno, it had taken some time and a lot of good-natured attention by Bruno himself.

Susan leaned over to me and whispered, "Artie would be so pleased!"

"Yes, but I'm sure he would have thought of a few things they forgot to mention," I said.

Bobby snickered.

I was watching the woman in the second pew again. She seemed to be shaking her head ever so slightly as some of Artie's stellar qualities were extolled. This made me even more curious as to who she was. She turned so our eyes met briefly, and she nodded and smiled.

I steeled myself as we were leaving the church, preparing to have to express my condolences to Tori. However, by the time Susan and Bobby Wang and I reached the doorway, Tori had already been whisked away, and she was being helped into the waiting limo.

We stopped to chat with Rachel Harwood and Malcolm Devlin, Artie's other partners in the medical practice. Rachel, a towering blonde with a reedy voice, was showing her middle age for the first time since I'd known her. Her face looked pale, she had smudges of dark under her reddened eyes, and she held her hands clasped to her chest. She seemed to be focusing on the hearse as the funeral director closed the rear door, and one of his associates began to line up the cars behind it and the limo containing Tori.

I gently touched Rachel's arm and felt her flinch as if I'd startled her. "Are you all right?"

"I just don't know what is going to happen now! I'm worried about how we're ever going to cover Artie's patient load. It was quite impressive; I don't know how we're going to absorb it." She looked from Malcolm to Bobby Wang.

"I know. God rest his soul and all, but dammit, Artie!" Malcolm glanced over at me. "Sorry, Melanie. But you know what I mean, don't you? The man should have known how to keep his—thing—in his pants!"

"We don't know for sure what was going on with the woman he was with," Bobby said.

Malcolm snorted, "Yeah, right."

"The police think it was a robbery. That's what I was told. Do you think it was something different?" Rachel asked. She seemed almost panicked by the possibility it could be something else.

Bobby put up his hands. "Whatever happened, we need to come up with a plan for how we're going to proceed. But not now. First, let's bury our friend."

I looked around, and I realized the crowd had dispersed as people waited in their cars for the funeral procession to start.

Susan Wang turned to me, "You're welcome to ride with us to the cemetery."

"Thanks, but I think I'll just meet you there." I had decided I owed it to Artie to at least attend the interment, but I had no intention of going to the "after" and wanted the freedom to leave when I was ready. I didn't feel up to talking to Tori at this point, and I was willing to wager she felt the same about seeing me there.

I stood off to the side of the crowd gathered at the cemetery. The sight of Artie's casket near the prepared gravesite made my eyes well up again. I did have some good memories, and many of the good deeds that had been recounted were true. In spite of the way our marriage had ended, there was a time when I was madly in love with the guy. I would miss him. He'd stirred so many conflicted feelings in me, especially of late, but I knew there was no point in holding a grudge now.

I snuck an occasional look at Tori as the priest read the graveside prayers. Malcolm was standing behind her and leaned in once to try to whisper what I assumed were condolences to her, but the sister either by look or words caused him to back away.

Once the final prayers were said, and as I turned to leave, I nearly ran into the blonde woman I'd seen in the church.

"Excuse me, you're Melanie, aren't you?"

"Yes." I noticed her eyes were a bright blue and contrasted nicely with her tan. Now that I got a closer look, her skin was a beautiful bronze, and although she appeared older than me, she was not as old as I first thought.

She took my hands in hers. "I'm sorry, it must have been horrible for you – you found Artie, didn't you?"

"Yes, I did." I slid my hands from her grasp. "Forgive me, but I don't believe we've met."

She smiled, "I'm Lynn."

No doubt seeing the blank look on my face, she continued. "Lynn Krapaneck Duncan. Artie's first wife. I flew in for the funeral."

Wait a minute, what first wife? *I* was Artie's first wife. Wasn't I? "I'm sorry.

What are you talking about?" The smile had frozen on my face. As a matter of fact, I felt frozen all over, unable to move.

"He never told you?" Lynn took a couple of steps back, as if taken off balance. "But didn't you...how could he have...?" She looked toward the flower-draped casket. "Dammit, Artie!"

I was sure whatever shock she felt was nothing compared to mine. "I'm sorry, but this just doesn't make sense. He never said anything about being married before he married me, never even said anything to hint at it. That can't be true."

She looked at me like she was either sorry to burst my bubble or couldn't believe I was still so naive. "No, it's true."

"But...I never even suspected." Of course, I realized, it should be no surprise in light of how Artie had pulled the wool over my eyes when he first started cheating on me with Tori. Whether it was skipping breakfast, the funeral itself, or this most recent bombshell, I had begun to feel a bit wobbly. I would have sat down right there on the ground perched on a neighboring gravesite, my head between my knees, except that while we were giving Artie his final farewell, dark clouds had rolled in, and fat raindrops began to fall.

Lynn held her purse over her head, "Are you going back to Artie's house? I could follow you."

. "No, I really don't feel comfortable doing that." I took a deep breath, "However, I think we need to talk. I have some questions." Yes, a lot of questions, I thought.

"I haven't expressed my regrets to the widow yet. Maybe after..."

The dark-haired man I'd seen follow them into the church was trying to help both Tori and Zeta into the waiting car, but Zeta elbowed him away, and slammed the door before he could finish saying whatever it was he was trying to say. He scowled and backed away, disappearing into the cluster of cars leaving the cemetery.

"Something tells me you're better off not introducing yourself to Tori right now," I said.

Lynn glanced toward the vehicle, which was now slowly rolling away. "There's a diner near the motel where I'm staying. We could go there and talk if you like," she said. She told me where to meet her.

I had begun to think the things I didn't know about my ex-husband were beginning to outweigh what I did know. Or thought I knew. I reasoned with myself on the drive to the Guilford Diner that this Lynn could be a fake, that she had made up this whole first wife bit. But why would she do that? The sick feeling came back to the pit of my stomach.

I ordered tea and banana nut waffles when we were seated. Although I had no appetite, I didn't want a return of the lightheadedness I'd felt earlier.

Lynn ordered only coffee and fruit. She leaned back in her seat. "You aren't what I expected."

"Oh?" I couldn't comment on my expectations of her since I didn't know she existed until today.

"When I learned Artie was involved with a nurse, I pictured a busty, loose moraled, gold digger out to bag a doctor husband."

I really didn't know what to say to that and choked back my anger at being so wrongly stereotyped. "Why? What would....?"

She put up a hand to stop me. She had begun to blush. "I know. I'm so sorry to sound insulting, but it made me feel better to paint an unflattering picture of you. Now I see I could not have been more wrong. Please accept my apology."

I nodded, but I looked down at my plate and could only push my waffles around, trying to regain composure.

Lynn reached over and placed her hand on mine. "Could we start over? I have obviously given you a shock by showing up and springing Artie's first marriage on you. I guess I shouldn't be surprised he'd never mentioned me. Artie always did like to edit his version of things."

"But that is a pretty big omission. Even for Artie." I said.

She nodded and looked away. "It doesn't feel very good to know he revised me right out of his life, I have to admit. What did he tell you?"

I sipped my tea, "I knew he went to medical school and did a residency in California, came to Yale to do a Fellowship in Dermatology, and decided to stay. Not once did he mention or even hint he was in a serious relationship, let alone married before."

"Was *still* married." Lynn sipped her coffee.

The same feeling that this couldn't be happening I'd felt after finding the bodies engulfed me again. "You mean you weren't even divorced then?"

She didn't answer but settled back in her seat. "We met in college, freshman year. As soon as we graduated, we found a justice of the peace and got married. It was the old cliché; I'd work to support us while he was in medical school and residency, then it would be my turn to concentrate on my career. Of course, there always were a lot of unexplained phone calls, some nights when I could have sworn he wasn't supposed to be on call. You weren't the first one he cheated with."

I wasn't sure if her remark was meant to be a consolation or a dig. I nodded for her to go on.

"After residency, Artie wanted to do a fellowship in Dermatology at Yale. I didn't want to move east. I grew up just outside of Phoenix, and that was where I wanted us to live, where I would become famous as an artist. He agreed. At first."

I remembered the little desert landscape picture that Artie had always had hanging, first in his apartment, then in the house in Branford, and that he took with him after the divorce. The artist's initials were "L.K." I thought he had just picked it up out west somewhere. Oblivious. "Is that when you divorced him?"

Lynn let out a short laugh. "No. We decided he would come here to do his Fellowship, and I would move back to Mesa and study under an artist I'd always wanted to work with. The plan was that he'd look for a partnership in Arizona when he'd finished his Fellowship. Of course, in the meantime, he'd fly out west for long weekends, and I'd fly east when possible. It became less and less possible as time went by. Artie always claimed he would be too busy. We'd never see one another, so why spend the money. That sort of thing. At the end of his second year of his Fellowship, he filed for divorce. Partly my fault, I guess. I never should have agreed to maintain our marriage long distance."

I couldn't look up and chance meeting Lynn's eyes. I'd met Artie two months before he finished his Fellowship. I was new to University Hospital, right out of nursing school, and had come to work on a medical floor. My patient needed a dermatology consult. The Fellow who'd come to see her was very charming and very handsome, and had led me to believe, very single.

"I'm sorry. If I'd known he was married—"

"Don't be. As I said, you weren't the first young woman Artie cheated with. I'd had suspicions, of course, but I'm ashamed to say I let them go. I figured as long as he came back to me, I could forgive anything." She colored a bit under her tan. "Besides, I had a little fling myself. With the man I was studying under. No pun intended."

We both laughed.

"Anyway, that's long in the past. When Artie filed for divorce, I didn't even object. Afterward, I met someone and am married again." A cloud passed briefly over Lynn's features. "I have a career that seems to be taking off. Finally. Things have a way of working out, I always say. I didn't want to see Artie dead, though."

"No, neither did I." We sat quietly for a few minutes. I don't know what Lynn was thinking, but I was fighting any parallels between his meeting and marrying me and what happened with Tori.

"How long were you married?" Lynn asked.

"Seven years. He met Tori when she came to his office selling the latest magic potion. It didn't take long for him to decide she was in and I was out."

"Do you have any children? Artie had always insisted we wait until our careers were better established until we tried to get pregnant."

"No. No children." It had been hard enough to talk him into a dog. I thought Bruno would understand if I didn't mention him. While he had a near-child status, it was a bit complicated to explain. I felt a twinge of sadness, thinking of how much Artie had come to adore Bruno. While we were married, his love of the dog made me hope that one day he might relent on a child also.

A thought suddenly occurred to me. "How did you hear Artie had died if you didn't know anyone here in Connecticut?"

She shrugged, "Actually, I have a former college roommate who lives not far from here. We keep in touch, and Artie's murder was in the news. When she heard Artie's name, she called me to see if it was *my* Artie. I talked it over with my husband, and he agreed it would be appropriate for me to go to the funeral."

"Understanding guy."

"Well, there is a chance for closure here. Did I mention my husband Doug is a psychologist?"

I nodded. "Closure is good." I didn't put forth any of my own questions about why Artie was murdered.

Lynn leaned across the table. "So, tell me, what's Tori like?"

"Predatory." The word just popped out of my mouth.

Lynn stopped with her coffee cup halfway to her mouth.

"I'm sorry. I shouldn't have said that. I really don't know her all that well. What I do know about her is from our limited interactions and in talking to Artie. I get the impression that she is more self-centered than predatory. What Tori wants, Tori gets. I think that Artie may have finally met his match in her."

Lynn seemed to be suppressing a smile. "Forgive me if I'm wrong, but you don't like her, do you?"

I laughed. "Is it that noticeable?"

"Do you think her grief was all show?"

"No. As I said, I think she is extremely self-centered, but I guess she really did love Artie. And much as I hate to admit it, Artie seemed to want to get the marriage thing right this time, too." I cleared my throat, "Especially since it turns out he had more practice than I thought."

Lynn let my final comment pass. "You'd think he would have more sense than to be fooling around on the side with someone else, then, wouldn't you?"

I met Lynn's gaze, "Yes, I would think so." Did she sense something was not right in the whole picture also?

She slumped back against the back of the booth. "But then again, this *is* Artie we're talking about. At my cousin Beth's wedding, he was hitting on the mother of the groom and was nearly beaten and ejected by her three other sons. He, of course, had his own version. According to him, there was a total misunderstanding of his intentions. I barely spoke to him for a week afterward, but then he sent the woman flowers and an apology. He was extra thoughtful and caring to me also, and he won me over. As always."

"Yes, he did have that ability to get people to overlook his transgressions, didn't he?"

We both sat in silence for a few minutes. It was going through my mind that finally, someone had not overlooked something he had done. Or then again, maybe his luck had finally run out, and he was at the wrong place at the wrong time, as the police said.

We spent the next half hour sharing Artie stories, sort of our own private farewell. Lynn told me she had met Artie when she enrolled in a course at college that was titled "The Art of Anatomy and Physiology.' She thought it was a class on sketching the human form. It was not. She asked the good-looking fair-haired preppy looking guy getting the same book at the bookstore why their text had such a detailed description of the thymus gland. He explained her error. He also asked her out.

I refrained from mentioning my own meeting with Artie, now that I knew he was still married at the time. Instead, I reminisced about the time shortly after we were married when he tried to teach me to ski. After the fifteenth time he picked me up off the ground, nearly getting plowed over by other skiers, he suggested I might be better suited to sipping hot chocolate by the fire. We shared a few more stories, concentrating on the good times, the fact that Artie could be funny and spontaneous.

Suddenly Lynn looked at her watch and said, "I need to go, I'm afraid. My flight home leaves in a couple of hours."

When we parted outside the diner, she said, "I'm glad we had a chance to meet." She took my hand and at first I didn't realize she had pressed a small piece of paper into it. "My cell number. Let me know if there is any more to Artie's story I should know."

I guess we both were failing to feel a sense of closure.

Chapter Five

After my brunch with Lynn, I headed home. The dark thunderclouds that had rolled in earlier were starting to drift away, and the sun was coming out again. I had to check my work schedule for the upcoming week and had let a lot of the household chores go undone with the upheaval of the previous week. Cleaning the bathroom for once had the appeal of a distraction as well as a necessity. I was still reeling from Lynn's revelations about Artie. Despite it being an awkward situation, meeting my ex-husband's other ex-wife, I liked her. After all, we did have something in common.

As I got out of the car in my driveway, a dark blue Range Rover pulled in behind me. Bobby Wang got out.

"Hey, Mel, we missed you at Artie's house. I thought you'd be going back there."

"It's Tori's house now. I wasn't really comfortable with that."

"Yeah, I see your point." He nodded.

"How is she doing, anyway?" I had heard her wailing as her sister stewarded her into the car at the cemetery.

"She is appropriately broken up. She went on about how she doesn't know how she will ever survive without Artie. Pretty much what you'd expect under the circumstances."

"Did she mention anything about the woman he was found with? Have the police given her any additional information?" I thought maybe they would share information with Tori, even if they weren't making it public yet.

"No. If they did give her more info, she wasn't sharing it. No one seemed to have any information on who the woman might be either, or at least they were careful not to say anything in case Tori should overhear. And I haven't heard anything on the news either. Maybe they are having a hard time finding family to notify."

"Yeah, maybe." I could hear Bruno whining at the front door. "Come in, Bobby. I have to let Bruno out into the backyard before he has an accident."

I took Bruno out long enough to do his business, then rejoined Bobby inside.

He picked up the conversation close to where we'd left it. "Anyway, I have to say Tori was pretty gracious to everyone. Her sister, however—what a snippy bitch."

I laughed, "I thought it was just me. I had the pleasure of speaking to her the other evening." I put the kettle on to boil. "Instant okay? It's all I have. Or do you want something cold to drink?"

"No, nothing, thanks. I have to get back to Artie's to pick up Susan; she stayed to help clean up. I just came to ask you a favor."

"Sure, whatever you want." I laughed, "Within reason."

"Tori asked me if I would clean out Artie's office at the practice for her. The sister, what's her name? Zeta? Zena? is taking Tori back to Boston to stay with her for a few days. She thinks Tori needs to get away from all reminders of Artie for a while."

"What does that have to do with me?"

"I have to go to San Diego. There's a big dermatology conference that starts tomorrow, and I'm on one of the panels. I committed months ago, and I can't back out now. I haven't even gotten all my notes in order yet. I've been so distracted with everything that's been going on. I'm supposed to catch a late flight out tonight. Malcolm and Rachel are going to be overwhelmed with trying to keep up with Artie's former patients besides covering any emergencies with mine over the next couple of days. Could you possibly clean out Artie's office for me?"

I felt a moment of confusion; I no longer had the kind of relationship with Artie where I would be the go-to person to help settle his affairs. I was no longer his wife. That was Tori's place. And she and I certainly did not have any kind of amicable relationship. "I don't think that's a very good idea."

"Please? Renata has the patient charts under control, and as far as the rest, you'll know what to keep and what to get rid of. In spite of everything, you knew Artie better than anyone."

I almost said, "I thought so, too," but bit back the words. "How will Tori take it when she finds out I was the one to clean out Artie's office? Can't it wait until she gets back?"

"No. She made a big scene at the house about how every reminder of Artie tears her heart out all over again. She said she 'just can't.' Besides, quite honestly, we need to hire a new partner ASAP. We start interviewing next week, and it would be a plus if we could show Artie's office when we do. Rachel booked the painters for Tuesday." He blushed a little. "You know, life goes on and all."

It sounded very cold, but I understood what Bobby meant. While the partners would mourn Artie's loss, they still had a practice to keep up. However, once again, I'd been sucked back into Artie's life, whether I wanted to be or not. Then again, it would be an opportunity to sift through Artie's things and possibly find out if there was anything else I didn't know about my ex. I never wanted to be blindsided again by anything to do with Arthur Krapaneck.

"What about the police? Don't they want to check out Artie's office?" I asked.

Bobby hesitated a minute, then said, "As far as I know, they're still saying it was a robbery. Why? Have you heard anything different?"

"No. I just wondered, is all. So, you don't think it was the work of a jealous husband or boyfriend?"

Bobby shook his head no. "The police asked me that the day he was killed. If he had someone on the side, I didn't know about it."

"Okay, I'll do it, but what am I supposed to do with everything once I go through it?"

"Just box it up. I asked Renata to get you some boxes and keep them behind the front desk. Once you've gone through everything, you can just bring it here if you don't mind. I'll see what Tori wants me to do with it once I get back."

"All right, when do you need me to do this?"

"Soon would be good." Bobby handed me a key ring with two keys on it: the office key, and the key to Artie's office. "Thanks a million, Melanie. I've got to go back and pick up Susan. And don't worry, if Tori says anything about you being the one to clean out Artie's office, I'll make sure she knows it was my idea."

I walked Bobby out to his car, and as he climbed behind the wheel, he turned. "Artie was a jerk sometimes, but I know deep down he never lost his connection to you."

"Bobby, did you know…never mind." I'd started to ask him about Lynn but changed my mind. Maybe I wasn't ready to hear the answer.

"Thanks again. I'll call you when I get back from San Diego."

After Bobby left I went back into the house to find Bruno sitting by the back door. I could tell by the way his tail twitched and by the look in his big brown eyes that he was expecting me to grab the leash and take him for a walk. The keys to Artie's office pressed into my hand, and I thought it was probably best to just get Bobby's request out of the way.

"Sorry, little guy. Later. I promise when I get back we'll go out." At the sound of "out" he started to bark, and I had to go through a short routine of making him do his tricks and rewarding him to calm him down. I, however, was becoming less calm by the minute. I was overwhelmed by a combination of curiosity and dread at what reminders of Artie I might find.

There was a sign on the office door, a tastefully printed arch of roses around the words "Closed Today as We Mourn the Loss of One of Our Own." I used the key Bobby had given me and eased the door open. The waiting room at Highlife Dermatology was set up as an open area aesthetically arranged with floral print chairs and potted plants. The desk was behind a blonde wood curved countertop and on a normal day would be occupied by the two receptionists and Renata, who oversaw it all. Artie explained to me when they redecorated the office that they felt the open floor plan, with no sliding windows to close away the staff gave a more friendly appearance to the office. As I stepped into the waiting room, I could hear voices coming from the area where the private offices and exam rooms were.

"Look, even if I had the key to his office, and even if you are who you say you are, I can't let you in there."

"I just want to look around, see if there is something of Artie's I could have as a keepsake. He would have wanted me to have some token."

The first voice was Renata's, the second was also a woman's. One I'd only recently heard. I headed toward them. "Lynn?"

Both women spun around to face me.

"Melanie! What are you doing here? How did you get in?" Renata looked like she was hanging on by a thin thread.

"Dr. Wang gave me the keys and asked me to clean out Artie's office for him." I turned to Lynn. "I thought you had a plane to catch?"

"I decided to change my plans after all." She looked from me to Renata. "I'll catch you up later."

"I was just telling her I couldn't let her into Dr. Kranpaneck's office. You won't believe what she's saying, either." Renata said. "She *claims* she was married—"

"I've met Mrs. Duncan, and what she's saying is true." Renata's eyebrows raised in an expression that said she couldn't *wait* to spread this bit of info. Even dead Artie was the best gist for the gossip mill in this office. "Why are you here, Renata? I thought the office was closed today."

She went back behind the countertop and sat at her desk, squinting at the screen on her computer, adjusting it slightly and tapping the keys. "Well, I *was* trying to get more of these appointments changed. With two doctors—gone—for most of next week it's a nightmare trying to get everyone seen. I was on the phone with a patient when I heard hammering on the office door." She looked up at Lynn.

"Sorry, I saw the sign on the door and was just leaving when someone came out of the office down the hall. They said they saw you go in here. I really don't think I was knocking all that hard."

"But why did you come here? What happened to having to fly back to

Phoenix this afternoon?" I'd felt an immediate bond with Lynn after this morning, even with our connection being the same ex-husband. Now all I felt was anger and disappointment that she had lied to me.

"If you have the key to Artie's office, maybe we can talk in there. I know I owe you an explanation."

Renata had stopped every pretense of working on her rescheduling and hopped up out of her seat again. "If you're opening the office, could I pop in, too? We aren't complete in switching to electronic files. One of the other doctors must have taken home the set of keys I usually keep in my desk drawer. I think Dr. Krapaneck left one of the patient files I need in there before he was—um, died."

Lynn looked coolly at Renata. "Maybe Melanie could find it for you. We don't want to interrupt your work any further."

Whatever happened before I got there, it didn't look like Lynn and Renata had formed any bonds. I slipped the key into the lock, the two women lurking over my shoulder.

The office still smelled like Artie's cologne, and a wave of nostalgia washed over me. "Touché'. It always..."

"His signature scent. I know." Lynn stepped in beside me.

The faint fragrance of the cologne began to fade even as Renata bustled in behind us. "Here, I know what I'm looking for; I'll just grab it and get out of your way." She began to rustle through a short stack of papers piled on one corner of the desk, although it was easy to see there was no patient's file folder there. Before I could register where I might begin to sort things, she began to yank drawers open and flip through more papers. The phone at the front desk started to ring, but Renata ignored it and continued to rifle through drawers.

"Phone's ringing," Lynn said.

"The machine will pick up." Renata glanced up briefly, and then went back to what she'd been doing.

This quiet task, this final favor on Artie's behalf, *my* snoop mission was turning bizarre. "Renata. Enough. I'll bring you any patient charts I find."

"But, HIPPA confidentiality laws. You shouldn't be reading—"

"For God's sake, I know what a patient chart looks like without having to read the whole damn thing."

"Sure. Okay, I'll be at the desk." She continued to flip through a few more papers and then eased the drawer shut.

As she left, I closed the door and turned to Lynn. "Okay. Explain."

She threw her purse, a floral print cloth bag the size of a pillowcase, onto a chair and walked slowly around the room. She picked up a photo of Tori and Artie standing in front of their newly finished house, his arm around her shoulders with her looking adoringly at him.

"He aged well. He actually looks even more handsome than he did when we first met in college." She turned to smile at me.

I said nothing and continued to stare at her expectantly.

Lynn put the picture down and walked over to the small painting hanging behind Artie's desk. She took it off the wall and sat in the desk chair, looking at it as she held it in her lap. "I painted this. I gave it to him on our first anniversary."

"I realized after we met that the 'L.K' must be you. He used to have that in his old apartment, and then in the one we shared after we married. I never questioned where he got it." I had taken a seat on the other side of the desk.

Lynn sighed and looked up at me. "I wasn't totally honest with you today. Doug never said it was a good idea for me to gain closure by coming to Artie's funeral. He doesn't even know I'm here, nor would he care if he did. The marriage ended six months ago." She barked a short laugh. "Lack of interest on both parts. That's one thing you could say about Artie, he was always interesting."

I reached across the desk to touch her hand. "I'm sorry about the divorce. But why lie about it?"

"I didn't want to seem like a total loser; twice divorced, my first husband doesn't even mention having been married to me. In any case, I'm at odds and ends now, nothing really to go back to. I thought I'd stay a bit longer and take some time to think." She looked down at the painting again. "I'd like to keep this, if Tori doesn't mind."

"I doubt she ever even noticed it. Even if she did object, I think that painting belongs to you anyway."

Lynn retrieved her bag and placed the painting in it.

I cleared my throat, "You never explained why you're here, at this office, though."

"I really did just want to see if he still had this painting." She met my eyes, "And because you weren't totally honest with me either, were you?"

I broke eye contact.

"There's something that didn't seem right about Artie's death, wasn't there? You were sort of skirting around the issue this morning, but you think something else was going on. I want in if that's true."

"Why?'

"The same reason you do. As much as we both want to hate Artie and believe that he finally got what he deserved for being such a man slut, we can't."

I smiled, "I know. I always pictured Artie dying a horny old man, still chasing skirts fifty years from now."

"What is it, then?"

"Something wasn't right about the whole set up. Not that I took a long look or anything, but that woman just didn't seem like someone who was meeting her lover. She looked a bit rough around the edges. Not someone I would normally picture Artie cheating with."

Lynn nodded but said, "Could she have been a hooker?"

"It is Artie we are talking about, so I suppose so. But why would he arrange a tryst right before he expected to meet me in the same place? And if it was a hooker, who would want to kill them?"

"Well, maybe Tori."

I shook my head, "No. She suspects he may have been cheating, but she seems genuinely unsure what was going on. Plus, I think she would punish him in another way besides killing him. Something he would feel a lot longer than a bullet to the chest."

"I hadn't thought about it until Tori mentioned something, but he had been a little distracted lately the times we met to exchange our dog, Bruno."

"Distracted how? Like nervous?"

I shook my head. "No. Not nervous. More like maybe he had something on his mind, but I didn't really think much about it until he was killed."

She was quiet for a moment. "The police did say it was a robbery."

"*Could* be a robbery. It would have been a very neat robbery. I didn't get the feeling the police were too convinced, though they let on that was what happened."

"It does sound like something doesn't fit. Maybe there is something here that'll tell us what was going on." Lynn said.

"Let's see if he has any communication in his e-mails from the mystery woman." I felt a little guilty going through his personal e-mail, but it couldn't hurt him now, I reasoned.

I moved my chair over as Lynn moved hers to behind the desk next to me. "Do you know his password?" She asked.

"It always was the same as his license plate 'skndoc.' I'll try that." A message 'incorrect username or password' came up.

"Okay. What now?" Lynn said.

"Let me try this." I typed in "#1skndoc" and his messages popped up. There were fifteen new e-mails in his box, all from pharmaceutical companies or medical equipment suppliers, and a few conference notices.

Lynn had gotten up to stand, peering over my shoulder. "That's it? He hasn't checked his mail in five days, and all he has is fifteen e-mails?" she said.

I hit *old mail* "Zero. It looks like everything has been deleted." I tried *spam,* but even that box was empty. "All right, something is definitely weird here. Let's start with the stuff in his desk." I pulled open the drawer Renata had been going through. It seemed to be all articles Artie had downloaded: "Microdermabrasion" and "Botox – The Good, the Bad, and the Ugly."

"Nothing in here looks too promising, either." I dragged over one of the cardboard boxes and threw the papers from the drawer into it. "I'll go through these again later, see if there is anything worth keeping." I opened his top drawer and went through his junk tray, the place he tossed odds and ends. I threw handfuls of paperclips, pens and two memo pads donated by some of the pharmaceutical companies who dealt with his office in the box with the papers. I could feel something jammed behind the tray and pulled it out. It was an envelope that had my name scribbled on it. I ripped it open and peeked inside. It held a couple of scraps of paper that proved to be ticket stubs for "Phantom" on Broadway. We had gone to see it on our first date. I remembered how impressed I'd been that he had planned such a wonderful time. There was also a picture of us as we boarded our honeymoon cruise to Hawaii, and the fancy gold pen engraved with my initials he'd given me for our seventh wedding anniversary, but which I'd thrown at him when I learned about Tori.

"What's that?" Lynn had come over to examine what I had found.

"Mementos, I guess. I don't know whether to be touched that he kept something sentimental from our marriage, or to be offended that he kept it in his junk drawer at the office." I grabbed up the items off the desk, threw the tickets in the trash, and shoved the picture and the pen in my purse.

Just then we heard voices outside the office, and the door opened.

"Miss Bass, what are you doing in this office?" Detective Cody stood in the doorway.

"Dr. Wang asked me to clean it out. Why are you here?"

She looked annoyed at having to explain herself, but said, "Our investigation into the identity of the woman killed with Dr. Krapaneck has made it necessary for us to examine the contents of his office."

There was a man, another police detective I guessed, standing behind her at the desk, as well as Rachel Harwood, one of Artie's former partners.

Rachel looked agitated. "What do you mean? Why would you need to investigate anything in his office? I thought you said he was killed in a robbery. Now you call me..."

Detective Cody spoke as if calming a toddler. "I'm sorry Dr. Harwood, but it's become necessary for us to take a look at his files and in his office. I can't give you any more information at this point." She turned back to me, "So, why did you say you were here, again?"

I went through the story of how I came to be designated to pack up Artie's effects.

"And who are you?" she asked Lynn.

I spoke up. "She's ...a friend. She's helping me pack up his things. So, do you know who the woman is now? How was Artie connected to her?"

"As I said, we are in the midst of our investigation into the incident and I can't discuss anything at this time. I'm sorry, but you'll have to leave. I'll contact you when you can come back and finish packing up."

"Is it all right for me to take these, since I've already packed them up?" I pointed to the box I'd filled with the contents of Artie's right hand drawer. "They're just professional articles he'd saved."

The second police officer swaggered over and flipped through the box. "She's right. Just skin stuff." His face turned a delicate shade of pink, "I don't mean that kind of skin stuff—I mean dermatology problems."

Detective Cody seemed to be stifling a smile as she said, "Why don't you leave it for now,.You can pick it up after we're done here."

"But, as the officer said, they're only...."

"Leave them." All apologies had disappeared from her voice.

I grabbed my purse from behind Artie's desk, and headed for the doorway, Lynn close behind. The police officer stepped aside to let us pass.

"How long do you think it will be before you're through?" I asked.

"Call the station in a couple of hours. I'll leave word when you can come back." Detective Cody went into the office and closed the door.

Rachel was standing by the front desk now, rubbing her temples with bone white hands. "What a horribly trying day. Thank you for helping out. I'm sorry about that." She motioned toward the closed door to Artie's office. "I can't think what they want in there." Her voice sounded shaky, as if she too was barely hanging by a thread.

"How did you know the police were coming here?" I asked.

"The officer called to say they were going to be searching Artie's office. He said to meet him here with a key. I felt one of us should be here when they did their search. But if I'm not needed, I believe I'll go home and lie down." She left, shoulders slumped, and eased the office suite door closed behind her.

Renata was back behind the desk at the computer, again punching furiously at the keys, the phone to her ear now.

"I'll just keep the office key in case I need it when I come back," I said to her as I passed. She started to respond, but then whoever was on the other end of her call must have answered.

"Hello. This is Renata at High Life Dermatology and...."

As we were about to exit the outer door to the office building, I nearly ran into Malcolm Devlin. "Uh, hello, Malcolm. I'm surprised to see you here." I could tell by his breath that he'd been drowning his sorrows.

"Rachel called. Said the police were coming to search the office. I thought I'd better get down here and find out what they were doing. What are you doing here?"

I went through my story again.

"Yeah, that's right. Bobby did say he was going to ask you to clear out Artie's things." He glanced up the stairway toward High Life Derm's office. "Cops say anything about what they were looking for?"

"No. We had just started packing things up when they arrived. They were pretty closed mouthed about what they hoped to find. You don't know what was going on with Artie, do you?"

He paused for a moment as if searching for something just beyond his grasp. "Nope. But you know Artie didn't confide *everything* to me." He looked blearily into my eyes for a moment. "Too bad what happened. He was a hell'va doctor." He looked back toward the stairs again. "Guess I'll check and make sure they aren't making a mess up there, aren't aggravating the lovely Renata." He let out a guffaw, "No, they certainly don't want to do that!"

He was more plastered than I'd first assessed. "Malcolm, why don't I drive you home?"

He shook his head. "No, thanks. Maybe I'll just take a little rest in the chair in my office." He turned as he started up the stairs, raising his right hand in salute. "Scout's honor, I'll sleep a little before I drive home."

"He's another partner?" Lynn asked as we exited into the parking lot.

"Yes. He doesn't always know when he's had enough to drink, but basically a good guy."

As we parted to go to our respective cars, Lynn said, "You *will* call me when you go back later, won't you?" She gave me her cell phone number again and took mine.

I hesitated for a moment, but then said, "I'll call you, but we may not find anything interesting after the police get through. I could use some help packing up what's left, though."

Lynn shrugged. "My social calendar is empty, and there are some other things in my life I'd rather not think about right now." She pulled a set of car keys from her seemingly bottomless purse and walked to her rental car.

Chapter Six

Bruno was overjoyed to see me as I came in the back door of my house. I poured some food into his dish and raided the refrigerator for a quick meal of yogurt and fruit while he finished his dinner. I had gotten out of the habit of cooking much in the evening in the two years since Artie and I split. Bruno sat patiently watching me as I finished my own meal, and after I rinsed my silverware, I took him out for a long overdue walk. The evening was warm, but with a gentle breeze ruffling my hair as we walked. I felt some of the tension leave my shoulders, a tenseness I hadn't even realized I carried. I couldn't help but rehash in my mind the weird, and futile, visit to Artie's office. A quick soul searching, however, convinced me that there was nothing more I could do about it at the moment. Bruno and I were back home and were just about to turn into our driveway when my next-door neighbor, Karen, called out to me.

"Is everything all right? I was kind of worried this afternoon, 'cause I heard that little guy there barking and barking. I thought maybe you were expecting a delivery, something I could sign for. I looked out, but I didn't see anybody over there at your house."

"No, I'm not expecting any packages." Bruno never barked unless there was a good reason. I felt a little prickle of unease at the base of my skull. "As far as I know, there was no problem at my house. Thanks for checking, though."

She nodded. "Maybe he's just upset with, you know, him seeing what happened to your ex and all."

She had a point. Bruno was the only witness to Artie's death. Only living witness, anyway. I hadn't really thought about that before. I picked him up and held him as I stroked his head. "I guess he's going to need some special attention for a while."

"Well, if you ever need someone to stay with Bruno while you're out, my Jenny just loves him and will be glad to help."

I thanked her and let the now wiggling Bruno back down onto the ground.

My cell phone rang as soon as we got back into the house. It was Detective Cody.

There was no greeting after I said "Hello."

"Ms. Bass, just how far into the job of clearing out the office had you and your friend gotten?"

"We just started going through the desk. And some of the computer stuff."

"What computer 'stuff'?" She was obviously forcing her voice to be controlled, which was good, since I don't respond well to being shouted at.

"I logged on to check his most recent e-mails. They were just advertisements from pharmaceutical companies and some conference notices." I didn't mention I thought this was odd. Everyone has some personal communications on their work computers.

"And how exactly were you able to get into his e-mails?"

"Artie was not one to change his passwords on a regular basis, it wasn't difficult."

"You didn't print or erase anything while you were there? Because if you did, that might be construed as obstruction of justice."

I don't respond well to threats, either. "No. As a matter of fact, we had just started looking at his e-mails when you arrived. Was there something specific you were looking for?"

"And just why were you looking at Dr. Krapaneck's e-mails?"

That was a good question, one I didn't have a comfortable answer for. In the end, I opted for the truth. "Uh—I was curious. I wanted to see if Artie had been communicating with the woman who was in the car with him. To maybe see how he knew her. I was just being nosy."

There was silence on the other end.

"You've changed your opinion about what happened to Artie, haven't you?" I said.

"I can't discuss the investigation with you. You are sure you didn't delete anything from his communications?"

"There was nothing there except for what I already mentioned. Is that unusual? That there was nothing personal there? And so few e-mails?"

"As I said, I can't share anything at this point. If you have any information or suddenly remember anything that might help, please feel free to call me. Do you still have my card?"

"Yes. It's right here."

" Another reason I called was to let you know you can clean out the remaining contents of Dr. Krapaneck's office now if you want."

I ended the call and checked the time. It was nearly eight o'clock, and I'd had a very long day, but more than ever now, I wanted to get into Artie's office and finish what we had started. I thought again about the timing of what had happened the morning Artie was killed. Whatever had been going on between Artie and the woman before I found them, why arrange it when I was due to pick up Bruno? The only answers that came to me were that either Artie didn't expect to meet the woman, or he didn't think she'd still be there when I arrived. In any case, whether robbery or planned murder, if I'd arrived a bit earlier, I could have been the third victim. I jumped when my phone rang again.

"Hi, Melanie? It's Lynn. I know it's getting late, but I thought you'd hear from the police by now. Have you?"

"Yes. I was just about to call you." Not really a lie, since I would have thought of it in a minute, after I obsessed about nearly being involved in a crime of passion or opportunity. Whichever one it was. "The police just called, and we can go back now. I'd like to get it done tonight. But if you'd rather not go, I understand."

"Are you kidding? I want to go. Call it morbid curiosity, or a final goodbye to Artie, whatever. I still have the directions on how to get there. What time shall I meet you?"

I looked at Bruno, who had a "you're not gonna leave me again?" look in his eyes. "If you don't mind riding with a dog as a third partner, I'll pick you up on the way in twenty minutes. Guilford Motel, right?"

"Yes. Thanks. And I love dogs."

Bruno was all over Lynn when she got into the front seat. He nuzzled her hair, her purse, the back of her neck. To her credit, she just laughed and petted him. "Good boy. You're a handsome boy, aren't you?"

"Off Bruno!" I tried to squelch the tinge of jealousy I felt. I was not about to share another male in my life with Lynn.

"No, he's fine." She ruffled the fur on his neck and scratched his chin. "He's so cute. I'm surprised Artie agreed to you getting a dog, though. He never really had much of an interest in animals when we were married."

"It was a hard sell at first, but I have to say Artie did really seem to love Bruno once he got used to him. That was why we were sharing him after the divorce. I mean, I don't *think* it was just to annoy me that he insisted we do so."

The rest of the short ride to Artie's office, Bruno rode in Lynn's lap, looking out the window and panting. After I'd pulled into a space right near the front door, I unloaded a couple of boxes I'd brought from the back of my car. However, I hadn't thought about how we would get back into the building once we got to the office complex. I had a key to the office, but not the building. Det. Cody could show a badge and get someone to come open up at any time. I had to look for a light on and pray there was a janitor on duty. Lynn went to knock on the front entrance while Bruno and I went around to the rear. I nearly collided with two gentlemen in green jumpsuits with Purefix Carpet Cleaning emblazoned across the back. They were just locking up the back entrance. Bruno ran over, tail wagging, to sniff their shoes. Instead of stooping over to pet him, they shuffled back and gave Bruno a rather alarmed look, so I picked him up and cradled him in my arms.

"Oh, I'm glad I caught you. My name is Melanie Bass. I'm here because Dr. Wang in suite 222 asked me to clean out some things from Dr. Krapaneck's office. I have the key to that office, but not to the building." They looked at me, then the dog, and exchanged a quick glance, shrugged, and shook their heads.

"I just need you to unlock the outer door for me, please."

One of the men said, "Sorry, no English."

I started to move toward the door, but the taller of the two moved to block me.

I motioned as I said, "In. I must get in." The man shook his head again and motioned for me to step back.

"'Hola'." Lynn's voice came from behind me. She launched into what I assumed was an explanation in Spanish, the only words of which I understood were "doctor," "Krapaneck", and "gracias." Their conversation lasted a few minutes during which I watched their expressions as she spoke: at first wary, then sad, and then curious. Lynn turned to me. "Show them your driver's license."

I did as she asked, and both leaned in to peer at it before looking back at me and smiling. Or were they laughing? I decided it didn't matter. The tall one pulled out his key ring and unlocked the entrance to the building.

"Good work," I said as I followed Lynn up the rear staircase.

"Da nada. They were from the company that cleans the building. They said they have strict instructions regarding the security of the building, but once I explained the situation, they thought it would be all right. We just had to promise that if any of the other tenants ask, they checked our IDs before they let us in. and that we would turn the lock on our way out. Oh, and I had to swear that Bruno was a good dog and would not 'peepee' on the newly shampooed carpet."

The desk area outside Artie's office was quiet now. Renata's computer, as well as the other two on the desk were asleep. I ran my hand over the nameplate on the door before I unlocked it. It would be weird to think of someone else occupying that space.

I expected the office to be ransacked; it always looked that way on all the cop shows on TV. Instead, little seemed like it had been disturbed. other than the empty space on Artie's desk where his computer had been.

The atmosphere in the office was a bit different, though. One of the officers who had been here must be a smoker. The faint odor of cigarettes lingered, so I no longer smelled Artie. Still, Bruno let out a little whimper and made a beeline to curl up in Artie's desk chair.

I checked the boxes I had begun to pack earlier, and it didn't appear the police had found much of interest in them. The papers were more disheveled than I'd left them, but not much if anything seemed to have been taken. "I'll finish clearing out his desk; do you want to start packing up his books?" I asked Lynn.

We worked mostly in silence, Lynn calling out the name of a book occasionally as she found one that she recognized from his med school days. One of his textbooks fell open when she picked it up, and she said, "Gross. I'd forgotten how disgusting these medical texts are."

"I always thought dermatology textbooks were the most graphic, well next to abnormalities in human genetics—those are the worst. When I was in nursing school, I wondered about the old texts in the med library that showed genetic abnormalities—how had the families of those kids felt?" As I picked up a stack of professional journals a slip of paper fell out from between two of them. I bent to pick it up.

"Did you find something?" Lynn came over to get a closer look.

"I don't know. It's a note." I showed it to her. It said, "I have what you want. Meet where we met before." A date and 7:00 AM were scribbled in a different color ink.

It was the date he was killed. The hairs on the back of my neck stood up. Artie had asked me to meet him at 7:45. "This first part isn't Artie's writing." I said, "But it looks like he wrote the date and time."

Lynn took the rest of the journals out of the box and began frantically shaking the pages. Nothing else fell out. "So, what does it mean?"

"I don't know, but it sure doesn't sound like a love note to me. It sounds like someone, possibly the dead woman, was going to give, or sell, him something. But what? And why then? And why not come here or to his house?" I shoved the note into the zippered part of my purse.

"Shouldn't we give that to the police?"

"Of course. Tomorrow." I reasoned that if I called, they'd probably think it could wait until the next day. But mostly, I wanted to think about what it could mean. I wondered, too, how the police had missed this in their search.

"What about the receptionist? Renata? Do you think she would know why Artie was meeting the woman? She was awfully intent on finding something in this office earlier today." Lynn said.

"I don't know. I'm sure the police questioned her, but you are right, she was looking for something, and I don't think it was a patient chart." I made a mental note to call Renata and ask if she knew anything about the note.

"Let's keep packing. Maybe something else will turn up," Lynn said.

The office claimed to be working toward a paperless system, but there sure were a lot of files still in Artie's desk. Insurance forms, blank mostly, and referrals from other physicians, which I knew were confidential. I put those in a separate box; I'd have to let Bobby deal with the disposition of those. Lynn continued to pack up all the knick-knacks and memorabilia, shaking each one before she placed it in a box. Nothing more but a few dust motes appeared.

"Oh, how sweet. Do you think Tori made this for him?" She held up a needlepoint pillow that read "Love and Trust" written on two entwined red hearts.

"No. I embroidered that for him. Ironic, isn't it?" I'd forgotten about that pillow.

"Well, he still had it. That says something."

"Yes, but what does it say? He kept your picture also. A trophy for each wife?"

"Okay. Good point." Lynn lobed a plastic model of the layers of the skin on top of one carton, then came to perch on the desk corner near me.

"So, we don't really know why Artie was killed, only that he was probably not having an affair with the woman, as we originally assumed. That leaves the most likely theory that they were just unlucky and they were at the wrong place at the wrong time and were robbed and killed, as the police have been saying, right?"

"Maybe. But it still doesn't explain what she had for him." I sighed, "And it's not only Artie's death that's bothering me. Something seems weird in this whole office. Those cleaning guys seemed awfully nervous when they saw us."

"You're right, but maybe it was just because we appeared out of nowhere, and they were not sure we had any business going into the building."

I stopped stacking papers in the box. "You could be right. Maybe I'm just reading too much into everyone's actions lately."

She stood up. "Anyway, first thing tomorrow, I need to find another motel. Some craft show is being held in town, and the Guilford Motel is pre-booked." She chuckled, "If only I'd known, I could have brought a few of my paintings to sell."

"I have a spare bedroom. If you'd like, you can stay with me for a while." I heard the words I'd uttered as if they came from someone else's mouth.

Lynn's face lit up. "Really? Great! That way, we could go over these things one more time before Artie's partner picks them up." She bounced over and resumed putting the last of the shelf items in a box.

"Yeah. Wonderful." I reached out to rub Bruno's head.

Chapter Seven

The next morning I loaded Lynn's two suitcases into the back of her rental car while she checked out of the Guilford Motel. I already felt pangs of apprehension that made my breathing hitch. Maybe this was not a great idea. After all, our relationship, if there was one, was based on the fact we were both ex-wives of the same man. A situation that isn't usually a basis for friendship. Besides, I'd gotten used to living alone. It was one of the things I'd found I liked about being divorced from Artie. The Little Miss Helpful voice in my head said, "Oh, come on, it's only for a few days." Doom laden words if I'd ever heard them. And why *did* Lynn pack so much for a trip she'd planned for two days? My reverie was interrupted by Lynn's voice from behind me.

"Oh, you didn't have to lift those. I could have done it."

"No problem. Just follow me. I'll show you how to get to my place."

She paused before she opened the driver's side door. "I really appreciate this. You sure you don't mind?"

"No problem." I gave her the most sincere smile I could muster. This was going to be a little weird, and not just the finding out why Artie was killed part, either.

My house was originally a two-bedroom summer cottage. It had been winterized sometime in the seventies, and until I moved in and repainted after the divorce from Artie, it had retained its avocado green–harvest gold décor. What drew me to it was the view of the salt marshes across the road, and the five-minute drive to Hamonassett Beach State Park on Long

Island Sound. Even though I had been there over a year, I had just finished repainting the small spare bedroom right before Artie was killed, and I hadn't gotten around to putting the room back in order. Lynn helped me move the bed and dresser back in place, and we transferred the paint cans and tarps out to the garage.

"What a cute little place this is! And I love this room; it's so bright with the morning sun. Your house has a very positive aura." Lynn peered out the window toward the small fenced-in backyard. "What's beyond those trees and brush?"

"McMansions. This place would barely qualify as the pool house to those places. Artie's- I mean Tori's- place is like one of those."

"Ah. Do I detect a bit of jealousy?"

I laughed. "Not so much, anymore. Artie and I had planned to build what I thought would be my dream house, but after the divorce, he built one for Tori. I was a teeny tiny bit jealous at first, but I'm over it. This place is so manageable, and you're right, it has a 'positive aura' about it."

I had to admit I would not have wanted to live in the house Tori and Artie built. He had gotten his way and built in Madison, but away from the actual shore itself. I had wanted a large house, four or five bedrooms, a home office each and maybe a large deck where I could relax and watch the tide come and go. Neither of us had a lot of families but I wanted room for visiting friends and maybe a child or two if I could ever change his mind about that. What Tori wanted was a castle, with live in help. I did envy her the size of the property, though. She had plenty of room to grow things, if that had been her style.

"How about you?" I asked," Do you feel jealous? You know, about anything?"

She turned to smile at me. "Nope. Why waste time being jealous? And besides, Artie and I were done a long time ago."

"Good. Cause I feel the same way about Artie." I knew that that was not 100% true, at least as far as I was concerned. I was curious about Artie's marriage to Lynn, and maybe just a little jealous to find out I was not wife number one. Truthfully, I was stunned, and ashamed that I had been so blind as to miss such a big deception on Artie's part. I looked at Lynn and realized she was giving me the same speculative look I was giving her.

She blushed and laughed. "Yeah, well. I guess we can both work on that jealousy."

I smiled and nodded. Maybe this wasn't going to be so weird after all.

I had to do some afternoon and one evening visit for the agency. Also, Judy had relayed a message that Charlie Duggan had asked me to stop by and see him at Mayflower Hills, the rehab center he'd been sent to after his surgery. I showed Lynn where linens, towels, and food were located, and gave her directions to a local market should she need anything.

"Could you let Bruno out into the backyard every few hours? But if it starts getting dark before I get home, please stay out with him until he does his business. We have coyotes here, too."

"Don't worry. We'll be fine," Lynn said.

Bruno followed me to the door as I left, and I bent to pet him and say, "Watch the place until I get back," as I always did.

The afternoon went quickly. I saw two patients who had been recently discharged from the hospital after getting their diabetes under control, and who needed re-enforcement of the teaching they had received there. Eighty-seven-year-old Mrs. Cables had fallen off a step ladder trying to reach her "good" platter for her "famous" deviled eggs. That fall had happened before a Memorial Day picnic at her church, and it was the end of July and she was just now being discharged from the hospital. My final visit was to Andrea Deutch, a new mom. Her baby was a glowing orange – the result of breast milk jaundice and slight dehydration. I had to assure her that her son's chances of being accepted at Harvard or Yale would not be decreased because she supplemented him with formula until breastfeeding was fully established. Millie, our receptionist at the agency office, called to say my 4:30 was canceled, the patient had been re-admitted to the hospital, so I decided to see what Charlie Duggan wanted to see me about.

Mayflower Hills is a single story, flat roofed building. The grounds are well kept, and the interior clean and remodeled only two years before. More importantly, I had followed several patients who had been discharged from the facility and was impressed by the discharge program and instructions they were given to follow. After checking with Melissa at the front desk, I approached Charlie's room where I could hear him arguing with another male. Not the physical therapist, I hoped. He couldn't afford to alienate any more people, especially anyone so critical to his recovery. I rapped softly on the partially opened door before pushing it the rest of the way open. "Mr. Duggan? It's me- Melanie Bass."

"I see you finally got my message." He was propped up in bed, his arms folded over his chest, and his stump was elevated on a pillow. The other voice I'd heard was not Tim Long, the physical therapist, but belonged to a thirty-something man in a sport shirt, shorts, and sandals. He was tall with curly dark hair and a well-trimmed reddish beard and he stood with his arms crossed over his chest in a mirror image of Charlie. He smiled and seemed to relax a bit when he saw me.

Charlie must have caught me eyeing his visitor; he tipped his chin toward him and said, "This is my grandson, Justin. Pain in the ass just like his mother."

"Thanks. I bet mom can't wait to spend time taking care of you, Gramps." Justin extended a hand to me. "Nice to meet you. If you already know my grandfather, I guess there's no need to apologize for his behavior since there's little chance of it getting better."

"Don't call me Gramps, I told you." Charlie winced as he shifted his position in bed and squinted up at me. "First off, I'm sorry to hear about your troubles. The ex being killed and all, though for all I know maybe you're glad."

Justin was right, I did know Charlie Duggan or else I'd have been taken aback. "Thank you, and no, I'm not relieved that he is dead."

"Didn't think you'd be one to hold a grudge. I saw him a couple of times; did I tell you? Nice guy. He gave me some cream for my eczema. Something I never heard of, but it cleared it right up. Entertaining sitting in that examination room and waiting too."

"You found waiting to be entertaining?" I asked.

"Course not the waiting, but I could hear somebody getting chewed out over keeping records straight or something. There was a whole bunch of yelling sounded like it was coming from the doc's office. Whoever he was having the fight with must have been so riled up he forgot the way out. Walked right in on me in the exam room, grunted and walked back out without a please or thank you. Nasty looking fella."

"Nasty looking how?" I asked

"Scowl that could cut stale bread and three scars on his cheek looked like he'd been clawed by something. Dark alley looking kind of guy." He shifted in bed again, and said to me, "Anyway, reason I asked to see you is I want out of here. I thought maybe you could talk to the guy in charge here, tell'um I'm fine now."

His grandson let out a deep sigh. "Grandad, we discussed this. You aren't ready. You won't follow the therapist's instructions, and your wound is not healed well enough. The doctor said maybe in a few more days. Mom has taken time off to stay with you then." He gave me an apologetic look. "I'm sorry, Ms. Bass, he has been badgering me to try to get him released early, but I didn't know he was going to try the same thing with you."

My cell phone started to ring in my bag. I looked at the number; it was from my neighbor, Karen. I had forgotten to tell her about Lynn. Maybe she was concerned about seeing an unknown person in my house. I'd call her when I finished here. I hit the ignore button and replaced it in my bag.

"I'm sorry, Mr. Duggan, but your grandson is right. The closer you follow the doctor's orders and co-operate with your therapist, the sooner you will be able to leave. I don't want to see you right back in here because you were discharged too soon."

"Yeah, well, thanks for nothing."

"I'll check on you again soon, Mr. Duggan. And nice meeting you, Justin," I said.

When I got outside the hospital, I dug out my phone again to call my neighbor back. "Hi, Karen. Sorry I couldn't take your call before."

"Melanie? I hate to bother you, but something isn't right at you house."

"I'm sorry, I forgot to let you know someone was staying with me. So, it's—"

"No. I saw you carrying her things in earlier, so I figured out you had company. Your friend went out, and then after a little while, the dog started carrying on like he was on fire, but I don't hear him anymore. I'm a little worried because he was so upset. And I see a light on that wasn't on before your friend left."

"I'm through with work for today. I'll be right there." Karen had been known to overreact a little in the past, but then there had been that incident of Bruno barking at something on the previous day. I figured I'd better check it out.

"Should I call the police?" she asked.

"No, I'll check on things first. Maybe he was just upset at being alone." I hoped.

As I leapt out of the car and approached my house, I could hear sirens in the distance. Karen hurried over. "I know you told me to wait, but the more I thought about it, I decided I should call the police. I think it was the safest thing to do."

I knew she was right, but I wanted to get to Bruno to be sure he was okay. The side door was unlocked, and I had given Lynn a key, so I didn't think she'd left it that way. Before I'd even gotten the door all the way open, I heard a sound between a yelp and a scream that sent a shiver down my spine.

"Bruno!" I stumbled over open books, sofa pillows, and empty cardboard cartons thrown around the kitchen and living room. I ran toward a whining coming from the bathroom.

I found Bruno inside a pillowcase, tossed into the empty bathtub. The opening of the pillowcase had been taped closed using adhesive tape from the medicine cabinet. I yanked off the tape and gathered the dog into my arms. "Oh Bruno, what did they do to you?" I held his trembling body against me as he licked my face, still letting out an occasional pitiful whine.

I jumped as a voice boomed, "Police! I'm coming in."

"I'm in here," I yelled, carrying Bruno out with me as I approached the voice. I hadn't focused on what the house looked like in my haste to get to Bruno, but I started trembling also as I got a look around now. All the books in the living room bookcase had been thrown around, papers were torn from the boxes from Artie's office and scattered, and cotton batting covered the disheveled sofa cushions.

The police officer approached me as I waded through the clutter in the living room.

"You the owner," he referred to his notes, "Ms. Bass?"

"Yes." I clutched Bruno closer to me.

"That was a really reckless thing to do—coming into the house when you didn't know if an intruder was still here. You should have waited for us to arrive." The look of righteous anger on his face was nothing compared to the anger and indignation I felt, however.

"Look, this is my house, and I felt my dog was in jeopardy. How dare—"

I was interrupted in my tirade when Lynn burst through the door, followed by another police officer.

"What happened?" She looked around the living room. "Melanie, I'm so sorry. After I unpacked, I went out to explore the area a little. I was only gone an hour or so. I'm sure I locked up when I left."

The officer, his name badge read "Bridges," turned to Lynn. "You live here also? I'll need your name."

Lynn looked to me, then said, "Actually, I'm just staying with Melanie for a little while. My name is Lynn Duncan."

Another officer walked into the living room from the back. "It looks like whoever broke in climbed through the back-bedroom window."

Both Lyn and I rushed to the room I'd helped her move into only that morning. There was little to disturb in her room, although her clothes were out of the dresser, and a blue mess was smeared across the hardwood floor where they'd dumped some of her acrylic paints. The window was open, and the screen pushed up. The air conditioner still sat on the floor in the corner. Lynn and I had planned to hoist it into the window this evening. White moths had begun to flutter in like snow in July. I started to close the screen but turned to the officer to make sure that would be okay.

"Yeah, go ahead. I just need you to look around and tell me what's missing. Probably somebody looking for stuff to fence for drug money. They usually go for small stuff. Jewelry, silver, an iPad."

I jumped when another form suddenly filled the doorway. "There was a plastic milk crate turned upside down under the window. Made themselves a nice little steppy stool to climb up." It was the young cop from the previous day at Artie's office. He nodded to me. "Hi. You figure out what they took?"

"No. I'll look now." I put Bruno down and said to Lynn, "You better see what you're missing, too."

Bruno followed me to my room, whining as we entered. My mattress was pulled halfway off of the bed, my sheets and comforter thrown in a corner, my dresser drawers pulled out and dumped onto the floor. A single shudder shook me. I only had a couple of really valuable pieces that Artie bought me while we were married. I only wore jewelry when we went out and in spite of the fact he always offered to buy me expensive pieces I preferred to spend money on other things. I kept what good jewelry I had in a velvet bag in an old shoe box on the top shelf of my closet. Not in plain sight, but it wouldn't have taken Sherlock Holmes to find them either. I dumped out my diamond engagement ring, a sapphire and diamond necklace, with matching earrings and a diamond tennis bracelet. Everything was still there. I checked the rest of my bedroom, then the living room again. A photo I'd taken and enlarged of two rowers on a nearby lake hung above the sofa. The glass was broken, the model of the layers of the skin from Artie's office on the sofa beneath it as if it bounced off the picture. The batting was from the pillow Lynn had insisted I reclaim from Artie's office. It was split along the front and turned inside out. I had my computer in the car, but my iPad was under the coffee table, lying face down but unbroken.

Lynn came from her room to join me in the living room. "I brought a silver and turquoise necklace and a pair of earrings to wear to Artie's funeral, but they are still here."

"I can't find anything missing either. Everything is just … a mess."

Officer Bridges made a noise deep in his throat and wrote something on his pad.

Officer Meyers, the young one, turned around shaking his head. "Anybody really mad at you?"

"No. No one I know of would do this."

Officer Bridges took down the times both Lynn and I left the house, and about how long we were out, then he closed his pad. "Well, right now, it's a break in, and vandalism. Let us know if you find anything missing. We'll be in touch if we learn anything or have reports of other break ins. Have a good evening."

I locked the door behind them as they left and came back into the living room to find Lynn shoving stuffing back into the embroidered pillow. "I think if you just sew up the tear on this, you could save it."

I took the pillow from her. The words "Love and Trust" still legible across the now slit hearts, seemed like a mockery. I crammed the stuffing and pillow into a plastic grocery bag and threw it in the front closet. "Thanks. Maybe I'll want to do that someday."

As we finished picking up and straightening things in the living room, Lynn explained where she had been when the break-in occurred. "I took Bruno out for a walk after you left, and then went down to the State Park. You were right, it is beautiful. I took a walk on the beach and sat down to watch the water for a few minutes. I stopped on the way back to get some more paint supplies and then came back here." She took a deep breath. "I'm sorry. As I told the police, I know I locked the door when I left."

"They must have come in the window as the officer said and left out the side door." I felt chilled in spite of the warm evening, "Do you want tea? I need to sit a minute before I tackle my room." As I passed the phone in the kitchen I noticed the message light blinking and hit the play button. Two messages. The first read "blocked number" and was just a hang up—probably someone selling something: cabinets or siding. The second was Karen Pulley's voice.

"Melanie? You there? I'm worried because Bruno is barking again. I don't see your car there." There was a brief pause, then, "Okay. I'll try your cell. When you get this message, call me, so I know everything is all right."

"Thank God for nosy neighbors, huh?" Lynn had come into the kitchen behind me. "Maybe I better go introduce myself to her tomorrow, so she knows who I am."

"Yeah. Good idea." I told her what Karen had said the other day. "She stopped me the day of Artie's funeral and said she'd heard Bruno barking like he was upset. Do you think it was somebody trying to break in that day, also?" The hang up call took on a more sinister tone.

"Maybe." Lynn seemed to shudder now. "What are they after?"

"In spite of what the police said, I don't think it was jewelry. It looks like it was something specific, because they didn't take anything of value. They dumped out all the stuff we took from Artie's office, so maybe it was something they expected to find there."

"And when they didn't, they started looking in places where they thought it might be hidden," she said.

"Question is, did they find it? Or did Karen's phone message scare them away before they could? And do they think we still have it?" The tea kettle began to whistle, and I took two mugs down from the cabinet.

"Do you have any idea what it could be?" Lynn asked.

I shook my head, "Even more reason to think Artie and the woman were not just killed in some random robbery." I remembered the note we'd found saying, "I have what you want." My hands shook a little as I set the mugs on the table.

I noticed Lynn took her tea the same way I did, a dribble of milk and no sugar.

Eerie, the small resemblances between us. "Whoever broke in was probably looking for the same thing we were—whatever it was that woman had for Artie."

"Yeah, but animal, vegetable or mineral?" Lynn said.

We sipped our tea in silence for a few minutes. I was exhausted, but figured I wouldn't be resting too soundly after the break-in. "I thought maybe I'd look at Artie's stuff again as we put it back in the boxes."

Lynn nodded "I'll help you." She pointed at the first pile scattered on the floor and said, "You take that half the room, and I'll take the other half."

I was two thirds of the way through my pile, and my eyes were starting to glaze over when I realized the last four or five pages I'd skimmed over were research protocols. Boring. Really boring. I wondered why Artie had kept them. He'd always said he couldn't understand the lab rats during his Fellowship who preferred research to treating patients. I was about to give up when I found one page of one of the protocols that had something scribbled in the margin. It was written in but then scribbled out. Most of the words were unreadable but I thought I could make out some letters that looked like "ter' or "ker." I could clearly make out the word "G. Goose" however. What did geese have to do with anything? Not your usual research animals. "Weird." I said out loud and looked up to see that Lynn had already succumbed to our stimulating reading. She was slumped over on the sofa, chin down and snoring softly. There was a sheaf of papers still scattered around her feet. I gathered them up, along with those that I hadn't read yet, and piled them in one of the boxes. Nothing I'd found had any meaning to me, and I decided I would look at the rest of the papers the next day to see if I could find anything that did make sense.

Lynn's eyes popped open as I gently touched her shoulder. "I'm sorry. Nothing here. Nothing that I could see, at least." she mumbled.

"Nothing much in my pile, either." I thought about the research protocols. "Just more myths about Artie dispelled. I don't think we have whatever the intruder was after. We might as well go to bed."

I was right about the kind of night I was in for. I put my bedroom back the way it was before it was trashed, and I even took a few more of Artie's papers to read in bed. In spite of Bruno's comforting form next to me, I started awake at every creak the house made, and was glad when the sky started to lighten with morning.

Chapter Eight

I finally dozed off for an hour or two, but I awoke feeling groggy from sleeping poorly the night before. I figured a short run with Bruno would help me feel more alert. The weather channel predicted early afternoon thunderstorms, but the sky was clear for the moment and it was early enough that the air hadn't gotten too sticky. As I snapped on Bruno's leash, I heard the door off the living room that led to the spare bedroom open, and Lynn let out a loud yawn.

"You sleep at all last night?" she asked.

"Not much. You?"

"The same." I saw her looking at the leash in my hand, "You taking the little guy for a walk? Mind if I lock up after you leave? I'm still a little shook up after last night."

I tried not to let the relief show on my face. I was looking forward to having some time alone to think as Bruno and I made our way toward the beach. I was certain there was something Det. Cody wasn't sharing with me, and maybe that was connected to why my home was ransacked. "No, of course, that'll be fine."

"Tell you what, I'll make something for us for breakfast."

"That sounds great." I grabbed my house keys and shoved them in my pocket.

I had just gotten to the end of my street and was about to turn down a little lane where there were tiny one room rental cottages, when I noticed a car heading toward my house. It didn't say "police" on it but looked like every cop car I'd ever seen on TV. I turned so abruptly I nearly yanked Bruno off his feet. "Sorry, boy, this is as far as we go for now." Bruno trotted obediently behind me as I rushed back to the house. I was just in time to see Det. Cody climbing out of the driver's seat of the Crown Victoria.

"Detective, is there a problem?" I was slightly out of breath as I approached her.

"Good morning, Ms. Bass. I heard you had a break in last night. Are you all right?"

"Yes. I wasn't here. Luckily, neither was my house guest." I strongly doubted she was here to check on such a minor crime.

She turned around slowly as if checking her surroundings. "Do you mind if we go inside for a moment, I have a few questions for you regarding Dr. Krapaneck's practice."

I certainly still had few questions of my own. But why was she coming to me for information? "What about talking to Artie's partners, or Tori? Wouldn't they have more answers than I would?"

She started toward the house, signaling me to follow.

"I've already spoken to Drs. Wang, Harwood, and Devlin. Mrs. Krapaneck is apparently out of town and won't return until later today. I'll be talking to her also."

Lynn opened the front door just as we got to it. "What happened? Melanie, are you okay?"

I reminded Det. Cody that Lynn was a friend staying with me. As we seated ourselves around the kitchen table, I repeated for Lynn the reason the detective had stopped by.

"I really don't know what I can tell you that would help. Artie and I haven't discussed anything to do with his work since we divorced." I said.

She glanced toward Lynn as if assessing how much she wanted to say in front of her. I tried to think of a way to quickly fill her in on who Lynn was and that it was all right to talk in front of her. I was afraid my explanation would make it sound like an episode of Days of Our Lives. Lynn beat me to it.

"Lynn Krapaneck Duncan." She held out her hand, "I'm also a former wife of Artie's, and he hasn't spoken to me recently about his practice either."

Detective Cody looked back and forth at each of us, then made a "Humph" sound in her throat. She fished a small pad from the handbag slung over her shoulder.

"And how was your relationship with your former husband?" she said, leveling her gaze at Lynn.

"Distant. I just arrived from Arizona to attend his funeral. I haven't spoken to Artie in years."

Detective Cody stood considering Lynn for a moment, then looked at me. "Did he ever let slip to either of you that he might be working on a new project? Maybe seem excited or unusually worried about something going on with his work?"

"As I told you, he and I really only talked about Bruno." I saw her blank look. "Bruno's our dog. Other than that, we kept it to the usual pleasantries: how are things going? That sort of thing. I might have noticed him being distracted once or twice, but isn't everyone?" I said.

She scribbled a couple of words. "Notice anything unusual when you were going through his papers?"

I looked at Lynn, then back to Detective Cody. "Actually, I found a note, unsigned, stuffed into one of his trade journals."

It suddenly looked as if antennae were about to pop up out of her head, "Where is it? Why didn't you call me?"

"I'm sorry, I was going to. Tomorrow. I didn't expect you to show up today." I stalked off to get the note. Indignation seemed the best way to compensate for the guilt I felt. I should have called and left a message right away.

My guilt was replaced with confusion as I watched detective Cody read the brief note. She seemed almost crestfallen. "Was this all there was? No other communications or scraps of paper? Nothing that relates to patient treatment or orders for medications? Maybe invoices?"

"No, nothing like that. Why?"

She didn't answer my question but instead flipped to another page of her little notebook. "Did Dr. Krapaneck indicate he might be away for a while, taking a vacation or anything?"

"No. As far as I know, he expected to meet me at the end of the week, so he could have Bruno for a few days." Bruno heard his name and sat up, looking expectantly at me.

Detective Cody looked confused, then, "Bruno? Oh, yeah, the dog."

"Detective, I think we could maybe help you better if you gave us a more clear picture of what you think was going on between Artie and the woman in the car with him. Who was she? Do you know why they were together?"

Lynn chimed in, "We read the note. We know the woman had something Artie wanted. Do you know what it was?"

Detective Cody stood up and walked to the window, then came and sat down again. "I can't go into details because there is more than one agency involved in the investigation, but I will tell you the woman he met has a long history of criminal activity."

"What other agency? They were investigating Artie? Are you saying he was involved in something illegal?" I asked.

"I can't divulge any details, but there is that probability."

Lynn spoke up, "What was it? Something like insurance fraud? Was the FBI looking for him?"

I was stunned by the possibility of Artie being involved in something illegal. Obviously, he had no qualms about a sneaky and chaotic personal life, but as far as his professional life, he'd always been thorough and caring. Or so I'd thought. "Yes, what kind of illegal activities?"

"I'm not at liberty to say. But—"

"Then how do you expect us to help you? If we don't know what we are looking for, how do we know if we have it?" I had jumped up and knocked the chair over in my frustration, and I took the opportunity of righting it again to regain composure.

Lynn stood up and went to the sink to fill the tea kettle. "Tea or instant coffee, Detective?"

"Instant is fine."

I sat down at the table again, my hands folded in front of me. "Look, we're just a little nervous since it seems now that whoever broke in last night thinks we have something they want. Am I wrong in assuming they may be the same person who killed Artie and …could you at least tell us the woman's name?"

"Ms. Bass need I remind you that you are not a professional, and you can best help us by just co-operating and giving us any information," she paused and looked at me meaningfully, "or evidence you may have."

I took a deep breath to avoid saying again that maybe I could be more helpful if I knew just what was going on. "Yes, but maybe the woman's name will ring a bell."

Detective Cody also looked as if she was biting back words. "Her name was Janine Sykes, or at least that is the name on her most recent arrest record."

The name had no meaning for me. I looked at Lynn, who shook her head and shrugged."Do you think that maybe whoever it was that broke in here could have found what Ms. Sykes had for him?" I said.

She nodded, "It's possible, but to be quite honest, I was hoping they hadn't. I came because I need you to give me everything you took from Dr. Krapaneck's office. New information has come to light that makes us think that there may be significance to something we initially missed in the contents of his office."

I looked at Lynn, then back at Detective Cody, "We reviewed all his paperwork again last night, trying to figure out what the burglar was looking for. We shook out the remainder of his books. Nothing. No receipts, no more cryptic notes, no plans for atomic acne medicine. But again, we don't know what we should be looking for."

Detective Cody didn't seem to react to my attempt at levity, nor did she offer any more information on what Artie was supposed to be involved in. "I don't expect you to be looking for anything. As I've said, that's our job."

I suddenly remembered the research protocols I'd found. "I just remembered that I did find some forms on drug research protocols. They stood out because I never figured Artie was much interested in research. He used to keep up on all the latest treatments but left it to others to come up with them."

Her eyebrows shot up, and she sat up straighter in her chair. "Where are the items you removed from the office?"

"You don't need to take the mementos and photos, do you? They aren't of any significance to anyone else." Lynn asked.

"I'll need everything. Sorry." She reached into her handbag and pulled out a receipt pad. "I'll give you a receipt; they can be picked up as soon as we are through with them." She paused, her pen above the pad, "Shouldn't these items go to the widow, anyway?"

"Yes, of course." She was beginning to irritate me again, I hadn't wanted to collect the stuff in the first place, and now she was making me feel as if I'd overstepped my bounds in boxing it up for "the widow." "As you said, Tori is away. I was just keeping the things until she got back."

Lynn and I had put everything from the office back in boxes, separating the personal items from the paperwork. "It's over there." I pointed toward the pile of boxes stacked next to the sofa in the living room.

She hefted the first container, "Well, be sure to give Mrs. Krapaneck that receipt then, so she can claim these later."

I stormed into the kitchen and poured two cups of tea. When Detective Cody returned for the rest of the boxes, I said, "I guess you'll take a rain check on the coffee, then."

"Sure." I heard her grunt as she lifted the heaviest box.

Somebody really should tell her to lift with her knees, not her back, I thought.

I shut the door behind Detective Cody as she carried out the last box. Lynn was perched on the arm of the sofa, the pillow I'd embroidered for Artie in her hands. She held it up and grinned at me. "Oops. She did say everything—"

"Where did you get that? I thought I put it in the closet."

"The slit was not that big. I restuffed it and sewed it up. Keep it until you're really sure you don't want a memento of Artie."

She'd done a good job of repairing it. I looked at the words on the pillow again. The stitches made a line under the word "TRUST." "I would never have put something immoral past Artie, but illegal? Never."

"It blows my mind that he was being investigated by the F.B.I!"

"She never said it was the F.B.I, but who else could it be?" I said.

Lynn got up and walked toward the kitchen, saying, "What do you think he was involved in?"

"I have no idea." As much as I'd always claimed to not give a rat's ass about Artie after the divorce, I'd always felt I'd *know* if anything really big was going on with him. Admittedly, I'd not seen the signs at first when he started cheating on me with Tori, but I was blinded by love and denial then. I'd convinced myself I was much more clear eyed in regard to him since the divorce.

I sat down in the chair opposite where Lynn had been, the scene in the car where'd I'd found Artie and Ms. Sykes playing back in my mind. What had he wanted from her? And why meet her there? I tried to disconnect from the gruesome aspect, focus on anything else that I could remember, but drew a blank. There was only the picture of Artie, dead, etched in my memory. I was startled when Bruno jumped into my lap and began licking my face. "Okay, we can finish our walk now."

Chapter Nine

Lynn decided to come with us after all as Bruno and I continued our walk. I was glad of the company this time. We proceeded in silence, both lost in our own thoughts. I was processing what Detective Cody had said about Artie being involved in something illegal. Drugs. That was the obvious conclusion.

As if she was reading my mind, Lynn said "Do you think Artie was involved in a drug ring or something? Maybe selling prescriptions for pills?"

"Maybe. Prescription drug abuse is certainly on the rise. But that Sykes woman's note said she had something *he* wanted, not the other way around." I looked up at the sky, the storm clouds had become darker, and the thunder was quickly drawing closer. "Looks like we better hurry and get home before the rain starts."

Bruno started to bark and pull on his leash as we came into sight of the house again. There was a silver-colored Mercedes with out of state plates in the driveway. A tall dark -haired woman was standing beside it, leaning against the driver's door.

"Who is that?" Lynn asked.

"I don't know. It looks like Tori. But I thought Tori was out of town."

The woman was turned away, looking toward the backyard. She was dressed in slacks and a dark blazer. It was the outfit of someone who rarely ventured out into the summer heat. As we approached, she turned back toward us, and I could see she was holding a cell phone to her ear.

"That's not Tori," I said.

I bent to pick up Bruno, and he calmed to an occasional "yip" as we approached the woman.

She quickly tapped her cell phone off and slipped it into a small purse she had been clutching under her arm. The hand she extended was bone white. "I'm Zeta Hauser, Tori's sister."

"Melanie. And this is Lynn." I didn't go into any of our former relationships with Artie: she obviously knew who I was, and I'd just let her wonder about Lynn.

Zeta reached out her hand again to pat Bruno on the head. "Of course, I know Bruno; we've met many times at Arthur and Tori's." Her smile never reached her eyes

Bruno drew back to nestle under my chin, just as a loud peal of thunder cracked over our heads. I felt a sudden warmth start to spread down the front of my shirt. "Bruno!" I quickly set him back on the ground and tried to pinch the urine-soaked shirt away from my skin. "Ugh! Please, let's go into the house."

I excused myself to clean up and left Zeta and Lynn in the living room. Bruno had followed me into the bathroom and sat next to the vanity looking up at me apologetically as I dried off after a quick shower. I made a mental note to call the vet about Bruno's sudden skittish, and unusual behaviors. I wondered if dogs could have Post Traumatic Stress Syndrome; he'd certainly had enough trauma in the past week. Meanwhile, I could think of no reason Zeta Hauser would be visiting me.

I could hear the conversation in the living room as I opened the door. "Yes, I've spent quite a bit of time in Tucson on business. There's a small cantina there, Rosada's Roost. Excellent Empanadas."

"Really? I'll have to go there when I get back to Arizona."

"What did you say you were doing in Connecticut?" Evidently, Zeta had not recognized Lynn from Artie's funeral.

"I'm visiting Melanie for a while. We have a connection that goes way back."

Both women looked up at me as I entered, Bruno following closely at my heels. "Sorry about that. Bruno's been a bit on edge ever since Artie's murder."

I saw Lynn had played hostess in my absence. Zeta was in the act of raising a glass of lemonade to take a sip. Instead, she put it down. "Yes, no sooner had we gotten back into town than the police came to speak to Tori, asking all sorts of upsetting questions. I think they should concentrate on the woman. I would never say this to my sister, but sooner or later, Arthur was going to get caught with another woman, and her husband or boyfriend would make him pay the price."

"Is that what you think happened? A jealous husband?" I asked. Zeta seemed very sure of her theory, and while I had good reason to jump to that conclusion, I wondered why she was so quick to think he would cheat on Tori.

"Yes. He had quite a reputation in the past, from what I've heard, and why else would he be killed?" She took a sip of lemonade. "After all, I can't think of anyone else who'd want him dead, can you?"

"No. You're right. Unless it was a robbery, as first thought." If Tori didn't know or didn't tell Zeta that Artie might be involved in something illegal, I didn't want to share any thoughts on the matter. I gave Lynn a warning look.

Zeta stood up. "In any case, I won't keep you. Tori asked me to collect the items you took from Arthur's office. Dr. Wang was trying to help, I know, but if he was going to be away, he could have just told me, and I would have done it for Tori. There was no reason to bother you."

I got the impression that this woman was in the habit of bothering whoever she wanted whenever she wanted. "Really, it was no problem at all." I felt a perverse pleasure in being able to tell Zeta and Tori that they were too late. "Unfortunately, Detective Cody was here just this morning and took everything I'd cleared from the office. It was mostly just papers and a few knick-knacks." I went to my desk, where I'd stuffed the receipt Cody had given me. "Here's a receipt for what they took. She said Tori could pick them up when the police are through with them."

The color had started to rise in Zeta's face. She snatched the receipt from my hand. "They could have told me when they came to speak to Tori, saved me a trip down here." She started to get up, but then sat down again. "What made them feel they had to go through his things again?"

I glanced at Lynn, who had shoved the "Love and Trust" pillow behind her back. She shook her head ever so slightly.

"I don't know. I guess you could ask them," I said

Zeta did get up then, rather abruptly, and said, "Instead of wasting time going through his belongings, the police should be trying to catch whoever killed Arthur."

"And the woman," I added.

"Yes, of course. That woman."

I was surprised the windows didn't fog from the frost in her voice.

"My sister is already distraught. This is going to add significantly to her distress." Zeta flung the receipt down and picked up the small purse she had set on the coffee table, and walked out without saying goodbye.

After the front door rattled closed, Lynn said, "Is Tori as lovely as her sister?" She pulled the pillow from behind her back.

"I always thought Tori was quite an arrogant bitch, but now that I've met her sister, I think that term has been redefined."

Bruno whimpered from his spot beside my feet and started to chew at his stumpy little tail again. I noticed he had already chewed a bald spot on the tip. "Bruno. Stop that." I guided his head away from his tail.

I got up to write myself a reminder to call Dr. Reddy, the vet, the next day. The pen I pulled from my purse was one with my initials on it that I'd taken from Artie's office, and I felt a pang of melancholy. It passed quickly, however. Detective Cody had all but told us just this morning that Artie was into more than just womanizing. I scribbled "Dr. Reddy" on a scrap of paper, and as an afterthought, Janine Sykes on another. The pen was the one Artie had given me as an anniversary present. It had an excellent heft to it. I was about to throw it in the junk drawer, but instead, I put it back into my purse. I'd ask around and see if anyone recognized the name Janine Sykes as someone who Artie had been having contact with. When I got back to the living room, I saw that Lynn was way ahead of me.

"I hope you don't mind." Lynn was at the computer. "Do you think she spelled Sykes with a 'y' or an 'I'? Let's see what Google has to say."

There was a Janine Sykes in Bethesda, MD, and a Jeannie Sikes in Andover,

MA. Neither one sounded like our girl. "Weird," I said. "The cops had info on her, though. Let's try court dates."

We hit pay dirt. Janine P. Sykes, a.k.a Sandra Wordson, a.k.a Lorainne Furst, had a missed court date two weeks before. She also had missed her date three times previously. "Says here she's wanted for failure to appear, possession of an illegal substance, possession with intent to sell, forgery, and B.and E. She sounds like a real charmer. What was Artie doing with her?"

Lynn closed the web page. "I don't know, but she was wanted for Breaking and Entering, and someone broke in here yesterday—"

"Yes, but she's dead."

"True. But do you suppose she was working alone?"

"That's a good point." The thought gave me a creepy feeling again.

"Zeta sure doesn't like her," Lynn said.

"Yeah, but is it because she and Tori believe Artie was having an affair with her, or do they know the real reason Artie was meeting her?"

Chapter Ten

I realized once again how lucky I was that Judy Pelzer was my supervisor. She got a per diem nurse to do two of my Monday visits, so I could take Bruno to see Dr. Reddy after lunch. When I got home to pick him up for his appointment, he seemed his usual perky self. Although Lynn said she had noticed him chewing his tail twice that morning, so far, he'd had no more accidents on the floor or anywhere else.

As soon as we were situated in a room at Dr. Reddy's, Shauna, one of the vet techs, led Bruno away to get his blood drawn. It struck me that whenever something seems awry with human or animal, medical bloodletting seems to be in order. Of course, there was sound reasoning behind this, but it seemed ironic in my present mood. Bruno seemed none the worse for the wear, however, as he trotted back into the room ahead of Shauna.

Dr. Martin Reddy is a bear of a man whose love of his work shines in his eyes and in the way his voice either croons or huffs, depending on his patient's needs. Today he crooned. He gently stroked Bruno's head and ran his hands over his sides, peeking between hair follicles, as I related the terrible events of the past week or so and Bruno's apparent reaction to them.

"Poor little guy. What do we have here?" As he began to examine Bruno's tail, the dog began to yip, and let loose a stream of urine. We both jumped back in time to spare our shoes, and Bruno cowered in apparent humiliation. "Sorry, Bruno, I didn't mean to upset you." Dr. Reddy placed Bruno on the floor again and stripped off his gloves. "I don't see any tick or flea infestation, and the rest of his skin looks healthy. His tail seems to be the only spot he is chewing so far. Of course, I'll want to review the bloodwork, but in the meantime, I'll give you some ointment to apply to the raw tail. I can also prescribe some mild tranquilizers, and if that doesn't work, maybe try steroids. I'd say that the loss of bladder control and chewing are probably related to stress." He cleared his throat, "He may just need some time to get over recent events in his life, but I think it would also be wise to see somebody who may be able to help him over this rough patch."

"See somebody? What do you mean? Like an animal psychiatrist?"

"No, not a psychiatrist, but, yes, a therapist. The focus is on helping the owners understand and modify their pet's behavior. It is very helpful in instances of abuse, new owners, or other instances of trauma such as Bruno has experienced." He must have seen the skepticism on my face. "I really think it's worth a try."

"Okay, so who do you recommend?" As he said, it was worth a try, and if it turned out to be bogus, well, I didn't see how it could make Bruno any worse.

Dr. Reddy pulled a business card from his front shirt pocket. "I am not getting any younger, and my practice is growing. I am going to be phasing into part time and have joined practices with another vet in the area." He handed me the card. "Dr. McKenzie is trained in behavior modification and alternative medicine as well as being an excellent veterinarian. I am looking forward to working with him. Give him a call. I'll let him know to expect it."

He bent to stroke Bruno again. "Don't worry, buddy. We'll take care of you."

As I climbed back into my car, I felt a sudden fierce flash of anger. Bruno is small, but not easily terrorized. Blast whoever it was who had caused this change in his behavior. I tried to hold back the tears as I pulled out of Dr. Reddy's parking lot. I didn't need a psychologist to know that what was bothering me was not only about Bruno, but about Artie being killed, the break-in, and not knowing how what happened to Artie led back to my door. I heard Bruno start to whimper again on the seat next to me, and I wiped my face with my hand and reached to calm him. Too late. He was going at his tail like it was a T-bone steak.

When we got home, Lynn was in the front yard painting. She had gotten a collapsible easel and some canvases on one of her trips to town over the past few days. She sat on one of the bistro chairs I kept on the back patio and was doing a wonderful job of capturing the marsh scene across the road. It was high tide, and a river ran through the seagrass, reflecting the blue of the sky. The tall stalks of yellow sea grass swayed as a breeze ran across the open space. This was a view that always calmed me. Her face was not calm, however. It looked like she had been crying. I noticed her cell phone resting by her feet. There was a smudge of amber colored paint on the screen.

"What happened? Are you all right?" She looked unharmed.

"It's nothing." She shook her head as if to clear it. "How did Bruno make out at the vet.?"

"First, tell me what's wrong."

She kept silently dabbing at the canvas in front of her for a moment or two. Then, "Doug called from Arizona. Seems he is planning on getting married again, and he wants us to sell the house we own there. I'll get my fair share of the profits, of course, but he wants the money from his share to buy a place his bride has her heart set on. We argued, and I sort of hung up on him."

I put my hand on her back, "Oh, Lynn, I'm sorry. I take it you don't want to sell the house."

"It's not that. I don't have a strong attachment to it. It's just that he seemed so happy, so eager to get on with his life. I'm still feeling adrift, trying to find what's next for me. Plus, even if I agree that it was for the best we went ahead with the divorce, I feel like such a failure!" She wiped her eyes with the back of her hand, smearing a little pink paint across one eyelid.

I rubbed her back for a few seconds. I knew what she was saying. Near the end of my marriage to Artie, I had experienced a similar feeling. Even though it was clearly his fault the marriage was ending, I felt maybe I could have done something differently to save it.

She took a cleansing breath and added a few more strokes to her canvas. "You never answered me. How did Bruno do?"

"Dr. Reddy doesn't think it's anything physical causing Bruno's symptoms. He's referring him to a therapist."

"What? You're kidding, right?"

"Well, actually, he said he's a vet trained in behavior modification. It sounds weird, I know, but I'll try anything at this point."

"I knew someone in Sedona who did that sort of thing. They were always booked solid."

"Dr. Reddy gave me the card of a Dr. McKenzie. He said they were going into practice together anyway. I guess I'll call his office."

"Oh, speaking of offices calling, Renata from High Life Dermatology called. She sounded as if she was trying to keep her voice down. I had to ask her to repeat herself twice because I couldn't hear her. There was a lot of background noise, too, like someone was complaining or arguing. When I told her you weren't here, she sounded upset but wouldn't leave a message. She said she'd call back later after the office closed."

"Hunh. I can't imagine what she would want. Thanks." I put my hand on her back again. "If it would help to talk about things between Doug and you, I don't mind listening."

"Yes, well, I think it's past that point. Thank you, though."

I went inside and began to make iced tea to have with dinner. The puttering around helped dispel some of the anxiety I felt over recent events. It seemed I was surrounded by problems I had no easy answer for. I felt bad for Lynn but knew that nothing would really help until she worked through the pain herself. I thought back to when I realized my marriage to Artie was over. I was angry at him for his infidelity, but also felt such an overwhelming sense of loss. Also, I felt indignation that he seemed to have so easily moved on. Lynn had to have gone through the same thing when Artie married me, and now she was going through it again with the death of yet another marriage.

I thought of making comfort food for dinner but realized I didn't know Lynn well enough yet to memorize her favorite foods. Instead I fixed her a glass of the iced tea I'd made, decorated it with a curly lemon peel, and carried it out to her.

Bruno followed me out, trotting behind me. "Here. You look like you can use this." I handed her the sweating glass. "Unless, of course, you'd like something stronger?"

She smiled at me. "No, this is fine. Thank you." After she'd taken a sip, she said, "So what did the dog shrink say? When will you see him?"

"Oh. I haven't called yet." Just then, Bruno plopped down and began to chew his tail. "Ok. I'll call now." I called to Bruno come with me, and we headed back into the house.

Dr. McKenzie answered the phone himself when I called. His voice had the ring of familiarity, but I couldn't place where I knew him from.

Initially, he told me he couldn't see Bruno until the following week, but when I gave my name, he said, "Miss Bass! I can't thank you enough for all you've done for my grandfather! He can be quite a handful, as you know, and you really seem to hold your own with him."

It clicked into place. Dr. Justin McKenzie was Charlie Duggan's grandson. I'd met him the other day.

He continued, "Let's see. I really am booked up, but would it work for you if I saw you and Bruno after my last appointment tomorrow? Say 6:30?"

I had a good day the next day. All my patients seemed happy and compliant with the care their physicians had prescribed. It helped me maintain a positive attitude also, and I tried to brush away the skepticism I'd originally felt at seeing a veterinarian trained in alternative medicine.

Dr. McKenzie's office was on the first floor of what appeared to be a double-decker house, with a grassy fenced in yard bordering the parking area. Bruno and I entered the small waiting room, and I took a seat in one of the blue vinyl chairs lining the wall. Opposite me was a closed door that featured a stick figure surrounded by cartoon dogs and cats. Below the picture were the words "Dr. (is) Justin." Cute. Bruno sat calmly, his head resting on my shoes as we waited. He made a move toward his tail a couple of times, but I firmly told him "No" and he gave me a pleading look but settled down again. After ten minutes or so, I got up to read the diplomas mounted on the wall. It turned out Justin McKenzie had a master's in psychology as well as being a Doctor of Veterinary medicine.

I turned as the door to the closed room opened. A woman leading one of the biggest Dobermans I had ever seen strode out of the inner office. The dog lasered in on Bruno like he'd just spotted his afternoon snack, but the woman immediately started making a weird clicking noise deep in her throat, and the Doby snapped to attention and marched out of the door at her heel.

Justin smiled and said, "Hi Bruno, Ms. Bass," and waved us in. To the right was an exam room with the usual stainless-steel table and counters and to the left was what looked like a consultation room or office. Justin led us to the office. It was set up with two comfy looking armchairs, a sofa, and a fluffy red doggy bed. I took one of the chairs and Bruno sniffed the doggy bed but came back to settle with his head on my feet.

Justin sat on the end of the sofa nearest me and Bruno. "Nice to see you again, Ms. Bass."

"Please call me Melanie."

He nodded, "Okay. Dr. Reddy and I aren't officially joining practices for another week or so, but he faxed over Bruno's chart. I'm sorry both you and Bruno had to go through such an ordeal. I can see now why he may have developed his worrisome behaviors."

He edged forward in his seat, closing the space between us ever so slightly. I felt the heat radiating off his arm and inhaled the very pleasant scent of his cologne. I wasn't sure how I should feel at this sudden invasion of my personal space, until I realized he was trying to edge closer to Bruno. "How have you been, with all that's been going on?"

It took me a second to realize that he was talking to me, not Bruno. "I'm all right. Just worried. About Bruno." I wished he'd stop looking at me. His dark-eyed stare was both unsettling and comforting at the same time. I felt tears start to well up again, and quickly bent to pet Bruno.

Justin bent too and started to stroke Bruno also. "I'm asking about how you are doing because I've found that many times it's the owners who cue their pets on how to respond to a situation."

I started to straighten up in indignation, but he said, "No. Keep petting him. In a few minutes, I'm going to ask you to slowly back away and see if he gets upset by me being the only one touching him."

I did as he requested, but still felt stung by him insinuating it was me causing Bruno's behavior change. "Really, I don't think any stress I'm under is causing Bruno to act this way. There have been upsetting times before, especially when Artie and I divorced, and nothing like this happened." I had completely stopped petting Bruno and was eased back into my chair.

Bruno not only let Justin McKenzie stroke his head but nudged over my feet more to get closer to him. Traitor! "So why did you decide to study psychology as well as veterinary medicine?"

He had also leaned back into his chair by this point, and Bruno was in a stuporous half sleep across both our feet. "Actually, it was the other way around. I planned on becoming a psychiatrist, but halfway through school, I discovered I preferred animals to people. No offense. I don't feel that way about all people." He looked like he was blushing.

"None taken." I smiled.

He cleared his throat, "So could you tell me a bit about how Bruno was acting when you found him on the day you discovered your ex-husband's body?"

I felt a heaviness press down on me at the thought of explaining once again what had happened that day. "He was frantic when I drove up. Cooped up in the back seat of Artie's car, trying to get out. So glad to see me." I stopped there for a second feeling once again the initial anger at Artie for being so foolish as to close Bruno in a rapidly heating car.

"So, you let him out. He must have been overjoyed, greeting you and pressing against you, giving you 'doggy hugs.'"

"Yes. He was obviously happy, but really intent on pulling me toward the Escalade where Artie—where I found…them." I flashed on the scene in the front seat of the Escalade again and clasped my hands in my lap. "Afterward, Bruno was shaking. He seemed very anxious. Maybe what you said is true. Maybe he picked up on how I was feeling."

Dr. McKenzie reached over and put his hand briefly on my clasped hands. "It's very likely he did. Our dogs are sensitive to how we are feeling, even when we try not to show our emotions."

"So, what do we do now?" I asked.

"It might help to notice what seems to trigger Bruno's anxious behaviors, is it specific people or situations? If so, we can gradually use "good" things, things he likes, to sensitize him again to the "bad" that scares him."

That did seem logical, and it made me feel less helpless in getting Bruno back to his old self. I nodded, "O.K."

He checked his watch, "Well, next time, I can teach you some relaxation techniques, in addition to the calm petting to use on Bruno when you feel he is getting tense, or if you see him gnawing his tail. I would suggest you keep him with you as much as possible. I realize you can't take him to work with you, but if there is someone else he seems comfortable with, you could leave him with them and teach them how to soothe him."

I was sure Lynn would be open to learning whatever it took to help Bruno, so that was one problem solved.

"Give it a couple of days where you use the calming petting and try to breathe deeply as you do so you are relaxed also. I'll put you down for the same time on Tuesday if that works for you." He said as he walked Bruno and me to the door. "We'll start on more calming exercises and a little behavior modification then. If that doesn't seem to work, we could try some herbal supplements or acupuncture."

I raised an eyebrow. "Acupuncture? For dogs?"

He laughed. "No, really. It works for them, too, just like people. Certainly, it's worth a try, wouldn't you say?"

I smiled, "I guess. Thank you."

I reached to shake his hand, and he held it a moment longer as he said, "I know it's rough to hear, but Bruno most likely will get better as soon as your life is back to normal and you're also not feeling as much stress."

I nodded. I hoped he was right.

I was buckling into my seat belt when my cell phone rang. It was Lynn's cell phone number. She was talking so fast that, at first, I didn't understand her. "What did you say?"

"I just heard on the news that they found a body outside the building where Artie's office was. It's a woman. The police haven't released her name yet."

Chapter Eleven

Renata had not called me back the previous night, so I reasoned I had a perfect excuse to call the office, besides my curiosity at what the heck was going on there. When I called the office line at High Life Dermatology, I got prompted to leave my name and number, someone would get back to me shortly. The office was usually open late on Fridays, so someone should have answered. Since I was going right by, I decided to pop in and see if Renata was there and what it was she wanted.

Bruno had finally settled down on the seat beside me. As I pulled into the parking lot at High Life, I noticed the wooded area at the right side of the building had been roped off with yellow crime scene tape. There were also several police cars pulled up around the building, as well as the Major Crimes van. A Channel Eight News van pulled out past me as I pulled in. My stomach clenched at the sight. I flashed back to the last time I had seen such crime scene tape used, and I consciously wiped the vision of Artie's and Janine Sykes's bodies from my mind. Now more than ever, I hoped Renata was in the office. Maybe whatever she wanted to talk to me about was connected to what happened outside the office today. Bruno hopped in my lap as I was about to get out of the car. Justin McKenzie had said to keep him with me as much as possible, so I grabbed him up and took him with me. Renata would vouch for him not being a problem. In addition to the police cars pulled up near the crime scene tape, there was a dark grey sedan that looked familiar. My recent experience with a crime scene had taught me the police would not welcome uninvolved people showing up during their investigation. I looked around to see if anyone was approaching me to ask what I was doing there, but everyone seemed to be occupied at the moment. I figured my best bet to get in to see Renata was if I avoided eye contact and just bustled along like I belonged there.

I ducked around to the back entrance of the building and caught the door before it closed when someone entered ahead of me. I waited two beats, then slipped in and tip-toed up the carpeted stairs as the elevator closed on whoever had gone in the building before me. The door to High Life Dermatology was unlocked. Friday evening was usually a busy time, since people tried to make an appointment after work or school and before the weekend. This time, however, the waiting room was empty.

"Hello? Renata? Is anyone here?"

The outside door to the waiting room opened again, and a police officer walked in. He paused, his hand still on the doorknob, and his face beginning to flame red. "What are you doing in here, miss? Nobody is supposed to be out here. All this evening's appointments have been canceled."

I saw him give Bruno the once over. "I was on my way home from an appointment with my dog. The office manager called and asked me to meet her here." A small exaggeration, but I thought it sounded logical.

"Is that so? And what time was this?"

I hesitated a moment, but then decided to tell the truth. "It was actually last night, but she said it was important."

He took out a small pad and a pen, "What is your name?" After I told him, the officer pressed his lips together and said, "Wait here." He motioned to one of the seats in the waiting room.

Bruno shifted in my lap and struggled to get down. He trotted up to the countertop where the receptionists usually sat, and stood looking up expectantly, his tail wagging frantically. Artie had always had the receptionists keep a bag of doggy treats in one of their drawers for when Bruno visited. He let out a quick bark just to let them know he was waiting, I guess. I bent to scoop him up again. "No, I'm sorry. No one is there right now. Let me see if mommy has any left in her purse." As I rummaged to find my baggie of doggie treats, I heard a familiar voice.

"Ms. Bass, what are you doing here?"

Detective Sunny Cody stood with her hands rooted on her hips. She didn't look particularly glad to see me.

"As I told the other officer, Renata Wells, the office manager here, called me last night, but I wasn't home. I stopped by to see what she wanted."

"Was she in the habit of calling you? Were you friends?"

I thought of the fight Artie and I had had when he hired Renata. I'd taken one look at her and made a judgment as to what she was really after. I'd never even thought of Tori back then. "No, we weren't close friends. But we get along okay, if that is what you're asking."

"Then why do you think she called you this time?"

I was becoming exasperated with her questions. "I don't know. That's what I'm here to find out. Look, why don't you ask her yourself."

Detective Cody paused for a few beats as if deciding how to answer my question.

"I can't ask Miss Wells. She is deceased."

There was a clunking feeling in my midsection. Renata dead? Why? "How? Is she the person who was killed here this afternoon?"

She raised a questioning eyebrow at me.

"It was on the news." Close enough to how I heard.

"So, I'll ask you again. Can you think of any reason that she may have wanted to contact you?"

"I'm sorry. I really can't think of anything." I meant I really couldn't think of anything. Coherently, at least. A lot of bits and pieces of what had happened over the past few weeks kept flitting through my mind. Detective Cody had said something else to me, but I had no idea what it was. "Excuse me?"

"I said, did Miss Wells leave a message when she called?"

I shook my head, trying to absorb that now Renata, someone else connected to Artie and the practice was also dead. "No. No message other than it was important she talk to me."

Just then, a teary-eyed woman, escorted by the officer I'd seen earlier, emerged from the back offices. She was another one of the receptionists, Bethany or Brittany, I couldn't remember which. She turned to the officer as they came to the door, "Could you walk me to my car? I'm a little afraid to go alone." He nodded after glancing in Detective Cody's direction.

"Do you think Renata being killed is related to Artie's murder?" I said.

"Do you?" Detective Cody asked.

"I just thought two people from the same office being killed within two weeks of each other might seem suspicious to you." It did to me.

"Mrs. Wells's purse was missing; we're looking into the possibility of a mugging."

"Isn't that what you said at first about my ex-husband?"

Detective Cody didn't have time to answer. The outer office door burst open again, and a very agitated looking Bobby Wang strode into the room. "What's going on? Rachel Harwood called me at the airport and said to come here immediately, that Renata Wells was found dead outside the office this afternoon. I want to know what you've found out so far. Who did this?" His gaze wavered from Detective Cody, and he seemed to notice me for the first time. "Melanie? What are you doing here?"

"You must be Dr. Wang." Detective Cody cut me off before I could answer. "Ms. Bass, I'll have to ask you to leave, but I plan on contacting you later. Maybe you'll 'remember' why Miss Wells wanted to talk to you."

"Would you please come with me, Dr. Wang?" She motioned for Bobby to follow her.

He said, "I'll be in touch, too." as he went toward the back offices with her.

I carried Bruno to the car and clutched him tighter as we passed Renata's Honda on the way to where I'd parked. He started to bark as I approached our car, and I looked over to see two officers by the area cordoned off by the crime scene tape. They were talking to another man. As he turned to point to the building, I realized it was Malcolm Devlin. He seemed very upset about something, waving his arms, and I could hear that he was raising his voice, but not make out what he was saying. Whatever the officer said back to him seemed to stop him in the middle of his rant. He stood with arms raised mid-gesture for a moment, and then he dropped them to his sides.

I placed Bruno in the front seat and slid in next to him. I wanted to know what Malcolm was saying to the police but felt conspicuous standing there watching them. I did stop, however, as I backed out to look toward the scene at the wood's edge one more time. One officer had Malcolm by the elbow and was leading him toward one of the squad cars.

I felt frozen in place, watching until the officer guided Malcolm into the back seat of his vehicle. What had he done? Were they even arresting him? I couldn't see how he could be connected to Renata's death. I'd had dinners with him and his now ex-wife Darlene when Artie and I were married. I was pretty sure he had always had "a thing" for Renata, I'd caught them flirting several times, and there were rumors when he and Darlene divorced that he had been sneaking around. I'd always wondered if it had been with Renata. In any case, Malcolm was a good doctor and a harmless drunk, not a murderer. I was startled when there was a rap at my car window.

"Miss, you need to leave." It was the officer I'd seen upstairs in the High Life office.

I hushed Bruno, who had started to bark again. "Sure, sorry." Once again, it seemed I was getting chased from a crime scene. I drove home, conflicted over whether I should even still be involved with the problems besetting High Life Dermatology. My connection should have ended with my divorce from Artie and certainly with his death and burial. Or so I told myself. But since his death, my home had been invaded, I had had several occasions to speak with the police, and I had Artie's first wife living in my house. There was no question in my mind that if Bobby Wang didn't call me later, I would call him to find out what he knew about Renata's murder and Malcolm leaving the office in a police car.

Chapter Twelve

When I got home, Lynn was in the backyard, sitting in a lawn chair, a sketch pad in her lap, and pastel crayons spread all around her. She was sketching the sky as the sun set. It was suffused with red and orange light; the wispy clouds tinted a light lavender. I had been so engrossed in thought over what was going on at High Life Derm that I hadn't even noticed one of the all-time best sunsets of the summer.

I let Bruno run around the yard sniffing and snapping at fireflies as I flopped into another chair and filled Lynn in on what had happened at High Life. At least what I knew about it.

"How well did you know Renata? Was there something going on between her and the guy they arrested?" Lynn stopped blending in a darker lavender shadow on one cloud to look at me.

"I have been out of the loop since Artie and I divorced, but I believe there could have been. I always thought she had a thing for Artie, but there were rumors about her and Malcolm, and at the funeral, she was hanging all over him."

"Maybe they had a lover's quarrel. Are either of them married?"

"Both divorced. From a few things I overheard Artie say, Renata was involved with someone, though I never heard who it was."

Lynn said, "So likely the mystery man was Malcolm, though it could have been some other guy who found out about Malcolm."

I laughed, "You're really getting into this mystery solving. Maybe you should think about a new career."

Lynn smiled. "Yeah, you're right."

Bruno ran up to plant his paws on my knees and drop an old tennis ball he'd found into my lap. I tossed it across the yard for him.

"Hey, that reminds me, how did it go with that new vet today?" Lynn said as she gathered up her pad and pastels.

"It was okay." I hesitated, thinking about what Justin McKenzie had said. "He thinks a lot of Bruno's problems could be a response to my stress over Artie's murder and the break-in here at the house. He's a nice guy, and it turns out he's the grandson of one of my patients. I'm supposed to see him again the beginning of the week."

"Oh?"

"No, I mean Bruno and I have an appointment on Tuesday." I couldn't help but feel a twinge of anticipation. I tried not to let that show on my face, however.

"Oh." Lynn put her things down on the kitchen table once we were back inside. "I've been thinking. You were right about me needing a new career, or at least a job. I'm not going back to Arizona just yet, and I decided to let Doug go ahead and sell the house."

I started to protest, to ask her if that was what she wanted, but she waved me quiet before I could get the words out.

"I told him to send me anything I needed to sign. I need to just get on with my life, make a new start. It's not as if I haven't done it before." She glanced at me.

I knew she meant her first divorce from Artie. But then, I'd had to do the same thing after he divorced me.

She took a deep breath. "I think it's time I started supporting myself, rent a place of my own and get out of your way."

"No, you're welcome to stay here as long as you want." I really meant it, too.

"That's a generous offer, and I appreciate you putting up with me at least for a little longer since I am basically homeless now." She laughed, but there was no humor in it. "I put up some notices about being available to give painting and drawing classes. We'll see where that leads. Meanwhile, I'll need to get something else to make money."

"Okay, well, I'll keep my eyes open for you, too."

I waited until nine PM to hear from Bobby Wang, then I called him. His wife, Susan, answered.

"Yes, he just got in. I'll get him." I heard her call to Bobby, and then she was back on the phone. "Isn't it terrible about Renata? The poor thing. Her co-workers got nervous when she didn't return from lunch. A patient for the Internist on the first floor found her. They say she was strangled and left in the bushes. Who would do something like that?" She made a sound like she was shuddering. "All I can say is she ran that office with a surgeon's precision. Like I told Bobby, I don't know how they'll ever replace her." I heard a voice rumbling in the background, then, "Okay, here's Bobby."

His voice was chipper, a little too chipper under the circumstances. "Hi, Mel, what's up?"

"What happened with Malcolm? Why was he taken away in a police car? Is he being charged with something?"

"He wasn't exactly 'taken away.' The police just had some questions for him, and they felt it would be better to do the interview at the station."

"So, he wasn't arrested?"

"No, of course not. He called me a little while ago to ask if I would come down and pick him up. He was all shaken up about Renata, we both were, so we went for a drink and then I dropped him off at his car."

It all sounded very reassuring, and his explanation would not have set off any alarm bells in my mind had he not sounded like Little Sammy Sunshine. "Don't you think it's frightening that Artie and Renata, were murdered? It sounds like maybe High Life Dermatology is being targeted for some reason."

Either he'd gotten tired of the façade, or I'd touched metal to a raw nerve, because the happy voice was gone. "That's crazy! Look, just leave the investigation to the police. We can't get bogged down in any paranoid notions; we have a practice to keep running. Don't think I'm not spooked, too. But I have to believe the cops are on top of it."

"I'm sorry, you're right." I waited a beat, then, "Bobby, there is something going on at the office, isn't there? Something besides Artie and Renata being killed."

It was his turn to pause a minute before answering. "Yeah, you could say that. Thanks to your ex-hubby, we all might get dragged down the crapper." There was a sharp intake of breath, "Look, I don't want to discuss it now."

"Discuss what? What did he do?"

"I said I can't talk about it."

I tried another tactic. "What was he doing in the car with that woman?"

"I can't say anymore. Goodbye."

Once again, a lot of questions kept popping up around Artie Krapaneck, "Can't you even…." The call was disconnected before I could press him any harder for answers.

I was exhausted that evening and fell into a deep sleep as soon as my head hit the pillow. However, I was awakened by a loud banging. Both Lynn and I came bolting out of our rooms at the sound of the pounding at the front door. Bruno was barking frantically, and I stepped in a puddle of pee by the door. I opened the door a crack and peeked out. Malcolm Devlin's red-eyed face filled the crack, followed by billows of whiskey-scented breath. I opened the door wider, and he stumbled in.

"Sorry 's late Mel'nie," His shoulders heaved in deep dry sobs. "Renata's dead." He collapsed into my arms, making me stagger backwards and onto the sofa as he pinned me with his weight. With my pushing and Lynn's pulling, we were able to roll him sideways into a semi-sitting position on the sofa. Poor guy, our theory about him and Renata having an affair must have been right. He tried to get up again, but his knees buckled, and he fell back.

"She's dead. She tried to warn him. Tried to warn…." He scrubbed his face with his hands and fixed me with a bleary stare. "She felt so bad. She figured out they were coming for him. He told her to delete—" He just stared at me blank-faced for a moment, as if he'd lost his train of thought. Then he began again. "She said she called. Too late. Told me to watch out." With that, his head lolled back, and he started to snore loudly.

I shook him hard. "Malcolm. Malcolm. Wake up. Besides the drinks, did you take anything else?" His slurred comment about Renata trying to warn

Artie alarmed me. He didn't budge in spite of the fact I was yelling right into his face. I gave him a hard knuckle twist to the sternum, a method I'd always tried to avoid, but one which helped to determine if a person was conscious enough to respond to deep pain.

"OW!" He snapped awake again. "Why'd you do that?" He rubbed his chest and looked around the room, his head resembling the sweep of a lighthouse beam. "If you know what they want, give it to them." He rocked back and forth, trying to get up, and made it on the third try. "Gotta go."

"What *do* they want? Who's they?" I tried to steady him by holding his arms, but he pitched back onto the sofa, nearly taking me with him again. "Malcolm, what did she try to warn Artie about?" There was no answer. His mouth hung open, and his eyes were at half-mast. He was breathing, but very slowly.

I shook him again, hard enough to make his head bobble side to side. "Malcolm! Wake up! What do you mean?" No response.

"Should I call a cab?" Lynn asked.

"No, we better call 911. I can't let him go home alone like this. I'm not sure he hasn't taken pills or something on top of all the alcohol in his system."

We only had to wait a few minutes before we heard the approaching sirens. Malcolm remained slumped in his stupor as I sat next to him, watching to make sure he was still breathing. Bruno sat trembling in my lap.

Lynn sat wide-eyed across from me. "What was he babbling about?'

"I don't know, but something besides the murders was going on at High Life Dermatology. Detective Cody made that comment about Artie doing something he was being investigated for, and Bobby Wang admitted it when I spoke to him." The wash of blue and red lights from the police cars and the ambulance, which had pulled up in front of the house, interrupted us.

Two burly EMTs heaved Malcolm onto the stretcher. I gave them his name and address and filled them in on how he came to be at my house.

After they pulled away, Lynn and I both decided sleep was out of the question.

I reviewed what Malcolm had said. Renata tried to warn Artie that someone was coming for him, and she obviously thought Malcolm was also in danger.

So maybe she knew who these people were. It sounded like she was the one to erase his emails. Maybe she had read a few before she deleted them. Why hadn't she told the police what she knew? Now she was dead.

Both Lynn and I jumped up simultaneously to check that the windows and doors were locked. As we returned to our seats, Lynn said, "What now?"

"I'd say look again in the things we took from Artie's office. There must be something there that means something to whoever killed him. But the police have everything now."

"Right, so whatever Malcolm thought you had, isn't here anymore."

I didn't feel any sense of relief in that, however. "Yes, but he still thought I had something connected to whatever Artie was up to. I'm worried he's not the only one who thinks that."

Chapter Thirteen

I decided to stop by Highlife Derm the next day to talk to Bobby in person. I called to be sure the office would be open, since they would be preparing to attend yet another funeral, the second to be held within two weeks. I expressed my condolences and shock to Bethany, the receptionist I realized must be the one the cops walked to her car the previous night, and asked if Dr. Wang was in.

"He's here, but I don't think he will have any time to squeeze you in today. Dr. Devlin is out sick, and Dr. Wang and Dr. Harwood are covering all his urgents as well as their own patients."

Yes, I *bet* Malcolm was out sick. I planned to pay him a little visit also after I saw my afternoon cases. "Could you please put me through to Dr. Wang's phone?"

Her voice held the practiced sympathy that came with the job. "I'm sorry, but he left instructions that only emergency calls were to be put through."

I smothered my annoyance at being shut out. After all, it wasn't Bethany's fault. "Okay. Maybe I'll catch him at home later." I decided to leave a message on his cell phone, making it clear he *would* talk to me at some point today.

Among the visits I had to do that afternoon was one to Charlie Duggan. He had talked his physician into letting him finish his rehab at home after his lower leg amputation. I planned to stop by to make sure he was monitoring his blood sugar, check his stump, and to evaluate his nutritional state. Wally Abbott was the physical therapist booked to work with him in the afternoon. I knew Wally to be a no-nonsense kind of therapist and wasn't sure if that would work with Charlie. Either he would recognize a kindred stubborn spirit, or he'd dig his heels in and refuse to do any of the stretches and balance work Wally would have planned.

Rex, Charlie's ancient Pomeranian, got up out of his chair to sniff my ankles as I came in. I figured he probably caught Bruno's scent on me.

"He likes you. He don't get up for many people."

"Mr. Duggan, you look terrific!" It was true, he had more color in his cheeks than I'd ever seen, and he was actually cheerful.

"Yeah, yeah, well, my daughter's been hovering over me like I'm a three-year-old." He didn't seem too displeased by all the attention. "She went out to the store. She was worried to leave me, she says, but I told her I didn't need no babysitter, and besides you were going to be here."

I almost was afraid to ask, but judging by his good mood, things couldn't have gone too badly with Wally. "How was your therapy today?"

"The fella said I did good. Comin' back on Thursday, said we'd do more work then."

I was relieved to see he was being compliant with his recovery plan. At least for now. I checked his vital signs, watched him check his blood glucose, and was very pleased to see how well his stump was healing. As I was jotting a few notes to enter into my charting later, he cleared his throat.

"Bad doings over at the skin doctor's, hunh?"

I looked up. "Yes, really horrible." I shook my head, "Hard to believe there could be another tragedy associated with the practice."

"I always liked that woman, Renata. Wore those blouses that buttoned down real low." He chuckled. "It did my heart good."

"Granddad, don't start with Ms. Bass now."

The voice startled me, as I hadn't heard anyone else come in. I turned to see Justin McKenzie standing next to an attractive middle-aged woman. He held a cloth grocery bag in each hand.

"Aw, she don't mind, just an old man's cheap thrills. What are you doing here?"

"I came to check on you and arrived just as Mom pulled in the driveway with the groceries," Justin said.

The woman held out her hand as Justin carried the groceries into the kitchen. "I'm Rita McKenzie. Glad to meet you."

"Your father looks wonderful; whatever you're doing is working."

"It's an ugly job, but someone's got to do it." She bent to kiss the top of his head as he tried to swat her away. "Excuse me while I put the perishables away."

As she entered the kitchen, Justin came back into the living room. "How's Bruno doing?"

"About the same. We had a bit of a disturbance at the house last night, and he came a little unhinged."

"Unhinged how? Is everything okay?"

I shrugged. "We're working on it."

"You could increase his sedative by one third if you think it will help. Also, I really would like to try the acupuncture. I know you aren't fully buying into it yet, but I've seen it work wonders in decreasing a dog's anxiety."

"Thanks, I'll think about it, but he was a bit better this morning. As far as the medication, I'm hesitant to keep him too sedated."

Justin nodded and looked at his watch. "Well, let me know if there is anything else I can do. It was nice seeing you." He turned to Charlie and said, "Granddad, I have to go. I have an appointment. I'll leave you in Mom's capable hands." He went to say goodbye to his mother.

"I also have to go, Mr. Duggan. I'm so glad to see you looking so well. Keep up the good work," I said.

He shrugged, but I could see a little smile start to form.

Justin came back from the kitchen, and we walked toward the door together. He waited until we were outside to ask, "How about you? Are you okay?"

He seemed genuinely concerned, and I blushed as I remembered what Lynn had suggested the previous evening. "I am going to be," I said. I was, too, because I was going to straighten out this thing connecting me to Artie. I was sick of it disrupting my life.

"See you Tuesday," he called as we both got into our cars.

I parked in the visitor's parking lot at Malcolm's condo and walked the short distance to number 11. It was a gorgeous summer evening, and I met several people dressed as if to go running as I approached Malcolm's unit. I nodded and smiled as a few people greeted me.

Malcolm answered on the third ring of his bell. He was the color of cold cream of wheat and shielded his eyes with one hand as he let me in. "Hi, Melanie, what brings you by?"

No sense beating around the bush. "I came to make sure you are all right, and to talk to you about last night." I tried to take shallow breaths as I got used to the smell of stale booze and sour body odor that permeated his otherwise tastefully decorated home.

He chuckled. "I guess I went on a bit of a bender, hunh? I hope I didn't act too boorish. Thanks for calling for help, by the way."

"Are you okay now?"

"Sure, a little Lactated Ringers via IV and a few hours to sleep it off, and I'm good as new."

I didn't point out that to say he looked like crap would be a compliment. I leaned back in the cocoa-colored leather chair I'd perched on. "I guess I'd better get right to the point. I'm curious to know what you meant when you said Renata tried to warn both you and Artie, and that I should get rid of the information you seem to think I have."

"What? Sorry sweetie, I have no idea what you're talking about." I noticed he refused to meet my eyes as he answered. "Like you said, I was pretty drunk. I must have just been babbling."

"Bull shit."

He placed a hand over his heart. "My, my. I don't think I've ever heard you swear before."

"Look, Malcolm, you seemed extremely upset last night about my having or knowing something that could put me in danger. I think that's the reason you came to my house, to warn me. You seemed to think maybe whatever it is had something to do with Renata's death."

He looked even more unwell, in spite of the fact I'd not have thought that possible moments before. "What exactly did I say?"

"First you said Renata tried to warn Artie, and you, about someone. Then you told me if I had what they wanted, to give it to them. I'm the one who has no idea what you're talking about!"

"If you don't know, then you're better off if I don't say anymore. Just make sure you didn't keep any souvenirs from Artie. He was a crafty bastard and didn't much care who he involved in his little schemes."

"*What schemes?* That's the problem. I have no idea exactly what he was involved in, so why don't you tell me."

A slight smile came to his face. "Afraid I can't, since the police and at least one other federal agency would put my ass in a sling if they found out I was leaking information about what was going on." Now he chuckled, "Good old Artie, turns out even I didn't know as much as I thought I did."

I got up and grabbed my handbag. "Thanks for nothing, Malcolm."

"Now, don't leave in a huff. You knew what kind of doctor Artie was, would do anything for his patients." He chuckled again, "And even more for himself. I think I know why he was with the Sykes woman when he was killed. The cops know, but they aren't making that info public yet. I think in this case what you don't know may keep you from getting hurt."

I took a deep breath, feeling beyond exasperated. "Why don't you let me make that decision? Why was Artie with that woman?"

Malcolm was guiding me toward the door. "You need to go. I have to get cleaned up."

I pulled my arm away. "I'm not going until I get some answers."

He sighed and said, "Let's just say it's a good bet Good Ol' Artie was about to leave those involved with his scheme holding the bag. I think the Sykes woman was providing him with some of the documents he needed to get away."

A thought occurred to me, and I instinctively took a step away from Malcolm. He wouldn't kill Artie. I knew that. But here was a strong motive.

He must have seen the look on my face. "No. I didn't kill him. I just figured out about how the Sykes woman was involved from some things the cops said when they took me in for questions after Renata was killed." He looked me in the eye and said, "True, I sometimes wanted to wring Artie's neck, and he would have left me in a very uncomfortable position when he left, but I loved the guy."

I nodded. "I know, Malcolm."

He took my arm again and gently nudged me toward the door.

"One more question. What about Renata? How was she involved?"

"You need to go. I desperately need a shower and something for this headache."

"Renata was looking for something when Lynn and I went to clean out Artie's office. Was she involved in this scheme?"

A look of pain passed over his face that I would swear had nothing to do with his headache. "Renata was ... great. She would do anything for Artie, for any of us, really. No. I don't think she knew exactly what he was doing, but I know she would cover for him without asking any questions if he asked her."

"Did she have access to Artie's computer? Was she the one who deleted his e-mails?" I tried to edge my way back into his place, but he stood blocking the way.

He hesitated briefly as he was closing the door, "Bye, Mel." He clicked it shut.

Chapter Fourteen

When I got home, Lynn was gone. I picked Bruno up onto my lap and petted him as I thought about what Malcolm had said, as well as what he had not said. The action of stroking Bruno seemed to be calming me as much as it did him. If Artie was meeting Jeanette Sykes because she had forged travel documents for him, that would explain why he agreed to meet her so close to meeting me. He didn't think the transaction would take too long. That meant that someone else knew Artie would be meeting her, and either wanted to stop him or wanted something Artie had, or they thought he had with him. Malcolm said if I had any information or access to any information about what Artie had been doing before he was killed, I should get rid of it or give it to whoever was after it. Good advice, except for the fact I had nothing left of what I took from Artie's office. The police had everything, except for the pillow I made for Artie and that had been ripped open in the break-in. Any secrets that had held would have been discovered. Then I remembered Lynn's painting.

I put Bruno down, and he pranced behind me as I went to Lynn's room. I felt a bit like a burglar myself as I went into her room but went right to the painting hanging on the wall. I felt along the edges, took it down and looked at the back, and finally re-hung it and stepped back to look at the painting itself. There was no information I could see in the desert landscape. At least there was nothing I could decipher. I'd ask Lynn to look at it when she got home to see if it looked different to her from when she first painted it.

I went back to sit on the sofa. Bruno jumped up into my lap again, requesting further massage. I felt another bald spot near his right rear leg.

I was sure it hadn't been there yesterday. I remembered Justin McKenzie's suggestion that I could increase Bruno's sedative if he seemed to be gnawing at himself more. After wrestling with my thoughts on drugging him too much, I decided it probably wouldn't hurt to give Bruno another half dose of Trazadone. That being done, Bruno fell asleep next to me. I thought back to the research protocols I'd seen in Artie's papers. There was the inscription "G. Goose" and the letters that were either a "ter" or a "ker." Neither gave me a lot to go on.

I went to get my laptop to check out recent journals on dermatology, looking for hot new treatments, or new drugs, anything that looked interesting or controversial. It didn't take long to make me realize once again that dermatology had the excitement of watching droplets run down a windowpane. I totally struck out with the "goose" entry. There were entries about "goose flesh" and "goose bumps," but nothing seemed to fit what I was looking for. I tried "ter" and "ker." I found over a hundred entries and began to slog through them. There was a mixture of articles published in this country and those from overseas. I skipped the ones that had not been translated to English, but that still left a hefty list of entries. After about forty-five minutes of this, I was about to doze off myself when Bruno jumped up and headed to the door, giving me the signal that he had to go out. I hit one more title on a list of European dermatology journals, and an article popped up: "KERABOLT: The drug of the future that can erase the past!"

After a quick trip to the backyard with Bruno. I read how Kerabolt, a drug developed in Sweden, was quickly replacing Botox as the treatment of choice in parts of Europe. It said the drug had originally been developed to treat psoriasis, but like many treatments, had shown to have other effects. In this case, it also improved skin tone and erased wrinkles and age spots. The company that manufactured the drug claimed it worked as well as Botox without having to be injected. That it was also very effective in treating acne as well as in reversing the process of aging. Although, they did admit the use in acne was still being evaluated. The article certainly made it sound like a wonder drug. There followed several more articles about how Borgenverg Enterprises could not keep up with the demand for the drug. Consequently, there was a waiting list with people paying exorbitant sums to be jumped up farther on the list. I was wondering why I had never heard of it. I felt a jolt of excitement. It was a long shot that that was what Artie was involved in, but if he had gotten access to this Kerabolt, it certainly would have been profitable. I searched further and found two articles from American journals, opposing sides about its safety and whether it was wise to fast track it through the FDA approval process. Since it wasn't yet approved in this country, that meant that if Artie was using the drug, he would have had to be in a test group or gotten it illegally. Could that be the something illegal that both Malcolm and Bobby had referred to? Were they involved also? Just then, the front door opened.

Lynn came in dressed in shorts and a T-shirt and carrying two shopping bags. Bruno jumped up and trotted over to greet her.

"Looks like you did some serious shopping," I said, motioning to the bags she carried.

"Yeah, well, I thought I'd better get some new clothes suitable for job hunting. What have you two been up to?"

"I was just doing some research; I remembered a fragment of a word I saw on one of the papers from Artie's office. I was trying to see if I could connect it to something that would explain what Artie was involved in before he was killed."

She dropped her bags on the coffee table. "Did you find anything?"

"Maybe." I closed my laptop. "I might have found what he was doing that was illegal, but I have to do more research before I can be sure. I also went to see Malcolm after work. He said that he thinks the Sykes woman was providing Artie with fake documents to flee the country before the Feds got him. That would leave whoever was working with him holding the bag. He also said that Artie left something behind that someone else is desperate to find, and that if I have it, I'd better give it up."

"But we don't have any of his stuff anymore."

We were both quiet for a moment, then I said," We know it had something to do with his practice, and we didn't find anything specific in what we cleaned from his office at High Life. But he had a home office. Maybe I should pay

Tori a visit tomorrow after work. Whoever is after this information may just be looking in the wrong place."

I had only ever been to Artie and Tori's house a handful of times, my choice. I was pleased to notice that I felt none of the jealousy now that I'd felt the first time I saw the place. A jealousy, I now realized, that had been more about the fact that Tori had gotten her way while I had not. I parked in the circular driveway in front of the "entranceway" to what was certainly now Tori's house. There were no other cars visible, but they would be pulled in the three-car garage anyway if Tori was at home. I approached the front door under a portico supported by six stone columns. A bit ostentatious, I thought. It must have taken about forty-seven dermabrasions to pay for those.

I could hear the bell echoing inside as I rang it and waited for five minutes before the door yawned open on a short olive-skinned woman. She gave me a polite smile and stared expectantly at me.

"Hello, I'm here to see Mrs. Krapaneck." I rolled the "R" in Krapaneck. It used to drive Artie crazy when I did that.

"Mrs. K is upstairs. Who are you? Police? She asked not to be disturbed."

"No, I'm not with the police. Please tell her it's Melanie. Tell her I just want to talk to her for a few minutes."

She waved me in but left me standing in the rather spacious entryway while she checked with Tori. The walls were pale lavender; I had planned on a more subtle shade called Regal Stone. The chandelier above my head looked as if it belonged in a concert hall, not a private home. But no accounting for taste, and I had no right to an opinion anyway, I reminded myself.

Tori descended the winding staircase, supported by her housekeeper. At first, I thought, "Oh brother, playing the grieving widow to the hilt." But as they got to the bottom of the stairs, I could see that Tori really did need to be held up. She tried to straighten as she reached the last stair, but instead bobbled against the woman supporting her.

"Hello, Melanie." Then she said to her housekeeper, "Elaina, please help me to the sitting room."

Tori had a rooster tail of black hair sticking up from the back of her head, and it looked like someone had tried to brush the mats out of her hair but had done a poor job. A green velour running suit bagged on her, and while it was air-conditioned in the house, it was blistering hot outside, so the whole outfit seemed bizarre. I followed her into the sitting room, the leading edge of a wave of remorse starting to wash over me. She really was in mourning.

As I sat opposite her, I noticed her eyes wandered, searching for focus, and she reached for a water glass on the side table near her chair, but her hand couldn't find its mark. Damn! She was either drunk or drugged out of her mind.

"So, what can I do for you?" Tori's words came out carefully enunciated, showing a microsecond of extra effort going into forming them. Tears suddenly started to well up in her eyes and drip down her cheeks. "Isn't this great? We're finally talking really nicely to each other after Artie is…dead?" The "dead" came out as a hiccup, and Elaina was at her side with a fist full of tissues.

"Are you all right? Maybe I could come back tomorrow when you are feeling better." As soon as the words were out, I realized this might be the best time to talk to her, when all her defenses were down, and the truth might just zip through the fog in her brain.

"No, no. I'll be fine. I'm just so sad, so sad." She grabbed her housekeeper's hand and pressed the used tissues back to her. "'laina, go upstairs and get my pills for me, would ya? I think I need to calm down again."

"No, Tori, you're calm enough. You don't need any more medication for a while," I said.

Tori dropped Elaina's hand and looked at me with a blank stare. "What makes you an expert?"

"I'm a nurse, remember? You have to wait a bit longer before you take more medication." I kept my voice soothing, cajoling. My professional voice.

She bobbled her head up and down. "Okay, maybe you're right. What were we talking about?"

"Artie. You're right. We should get along. We both loved Artie, didn't we?"

She nodded, and it looked like her eyes were filling up again. "I miss him."

"I do, too." Once again, I realized I meant that. "As a matter of fact, the whole medical community will miss him. Something came up the other day about how so many of his patients had great results with their restorative treatments."

She looked like she was starting to blank out again.

"You know, anti-aging treatments."

She nodded.

"I was wondering if he ever mentioned a drug called Kerabolt, maybe told you about this new drug from Europe that was proving to work better than Botox to treat the effects of aging?"

"No." She shook her head, as if to clear it. "Wait, maybe he said something about some drug. I can't remember. Not 'Karinbolts' though."

"Did he talk about going away on a trip? Maybe a vacation?"

She let out a deep sigh. "I would really like to go on a vacation."

So much for breaking through her mental fog. "Was Artie acting nervous at all right before he died? Did he seem as if he was hiding something?"

"Ha!" She threw her head back and almost fell out of the chair. "Artie always had secrets. Most times it was better not to know. Least that's what he always said." Her eyes narrowed as if she was trying extremely hard to focus. "Hey! Was he screwing you when you met for the dog?"

"No! I swear." What mental path had she just darted down?

"Okay. I thought maybe that was it." Tori slumped in her chair, and her eyes took on their unfocused look again. "I'm tired. Elaina, take me back upstairs."

"Just one more question. Was there a place Artie kept important papers or things that he wanted kept safe?"

The voice that answered was stern and came from the doorway. "The police have already been here and gone over all Arthur's effects, including his desk and home computer."

I hadn't heard anyone else enter the room.

Zeta came to stand beside her sister. "Tori, the doctor warned you not to overexert yourself, especially while you are on the medication."

"He said that? I don't remember."

Zeta pried her sister up out of the chair, motioning to Elaina to help. "I don't know why you're here, Ms. Bass, but I don't see that you have any right to butt into a police investigation, and certainly no right to harass my sister. Please leave."

I stood up. "I wasn't harassing her. We were just talking about Artie." I was butting into a police investigation, so I let that comment slide. "I hope you feel better, Tori, and if you remember anything, give me a call." If she remembered I was even here, I'd be surprised.

I hesitated as another thought occurred to me. Zeta might be more of a help than Tori, as she was still employed at Raffkin Pharmaceuticals. "Zeta, there's something you may be able to help me with. I've been reading about a new drug called Kerabolt, supposedly, it has excellent results, even better than Botox. What have you heard about it?"

She let Tori slip back into the chair a bit. "Kerabolt? Why do you want to know?"

I lied. "I have a patient who asked me about it, and I said I'd look into it for her."

She grabbed Tori up again, "Tell your patient to see her doctor. Everyone reads about these new wonder drugs, thinks all they have to do is ask, and they can have whatever they want. Kerabolt is what they are hyping now. It is one of several new meds under investigation, but so far, none are available in the U.S., so she's out of luck." She whipped Tori around, and half dragged her out of the room.

"Okay. Thanks," I called after them, but Zeta never even turned around. I wondered if Tori had a prescription for whatever she was taking, and if so, who wrote it.

Chapter Fifteen

I thought some more about Kerabolt on the drive home. I'd touched a nerve when I'd asked Zeta about it, that was for sure. It had to have been that or something like it that Artie had been mixed up with. Both Bobby and Malcolm had mentioned a federal agency that was involved in whatever Artie was doing. We had assumed it was the FBI, but maybe it was the FDA. I made a mental note to do more research to find out what the holdup was with the approval to use Kerabolt in this country.

I sat in the car for a moment after I parked in my driveway. I would like to believe Artie was doing a legitimate trial for the drug, but in my gut, I knew that wasn't true. Adding together what the police said and what I'd learned from Malcolm about Jeanette Sykes it was obvious that Artie knew he was in trouble and was getting ready to leave it all behind. But was the Sykes woman involved in any way with the drug, or was she just someone he contacted to get a fake ID to leave the country? It seemed that Tori didn't know anything about them planning to go anywhere before Artie was killed. But then she had never directly answered my question about a planned trip either.

Lynn was on the back patio giving Bruno a bath when I went into the house. "I hope you don't mind. I got this shampoo at Love the Dog today. It's organic and hypoallergenic. He was scratching so much today I thought it might give him some relief."

"Thanks, Lynn."

"I tried some of the soothing techniques you said the vet gave you also. I think it helped a little bit."

I noted with alarm how many bald spots Bruno had dug out on himself. "It's not fleas, or mites, or mange, or any other common skin complaint Dr. Reddy could come up with, but I don't know how a psychological problem could cause this much physical reaction either. I'll call the vet's office again in the morning."

I grabbed the towel from the chair and took Bruno from the little plastic wash tub, dodging splashes of water as he shook himself. "It's ironic, isn't it? Looks like what Bruno needs is a good dermatologist."

Lynn chuckled. "Speaking of which, how did it go with the widow Krapaneck?"

"We were civil, made all the easier since she was flying high on something her 'doctor' gave her for her depression. She could barely remember from one word to the next what either of us was saying. I don't think she knows anything about Artie's last enterprises, or at least isn't aware she knows it. I never got a chance to look in Artie's office myself, though. Her harpy of a sister interrupted us. She said the police had already searched Artie's office, and there was nothing left to find, and then she basically kicked me out."

"What was she upset about?"

"She didn't seem to want me talking to Tori. I'm not sure why. She also made it plain she didn't like that I'd dared to butt into a police investigation. Again, I'm not sure why she should care. I mentioned Kerabolt, that drug I read about on the internet. I asked if she knew anything about it. It seemed as if she did but didn't give me any more information on it."

"So, that's it? You don't think there is anything to find at Artie's?" Lynn crossed the yard to empty the tub at the edge of the gravel lining the edge of the privacy fence.

"No, I think there is definitely more to know there. Tori even made the comment that Artie always had secrets but told her it was better not to know what was going on. Of course, she took that to mean that Artie and I were fooling around when he professed to be dropping off Bruno or picking him up."

Lynn paused as she dried the plastic tub. "Well...were you?"

"No! Of course not!" I felt a sudden flash of anger mixed with betrayal. I'd made it clear, hadn't I, how I felt about Artie. "Would you have if given the chance?"

She smiled enigmatically. "Honest? I don't know. Maybe."

Not the answer I'd expected. I picked up Bruno without saying another word and carried him toward the house. Her answer flustered me, and I wasn't sure why. I told myself it was because it drove home the fact that I really didn't know Lynn well, only a couple of weeks, and she obviously didn't know me.

I put dog food into Bruno's dish, then started to pull food out of the refrigerator for dinner. Lynn stood by the kitchen sink. "Look, Melanie, I didn't mean to offend you by asking about Artie. I just meant that we don't always know how we're going to act in certain circumstances. If you had asked me a couple of months ago if I would sleep with Artie Krapaneck again, I'd have reacted much the way you did. Now, I guess, since he isn't here to remind me of what a jerk he was, I'm not so sure how I would have reacted if the situation arose. Maybe I was just remembering the good times. You have to admit Artie was a handsome man. He was also smart and could charm people into doing pretty much whatever he wanted."

And he knew it, too. "All right. I see your point. I do miss him in spite of his less endearing points, but believe me, I did not sleep with Artie after the divorce." I handed her the makings of a salad as I went out to the patio to put the marinated chicken on the grill. What she said about not always knowing how a person would react was true. It made me wonder if the person who shot Artie went there with the intent, or did something go wrong in their encounter with him?

The aroma of the chicken cooking mixed with the pungent odor of low tide in the tidal marsh across the road. I watched the seagulls dive toward the mud flats, easy pickings for their dinner tonight. There was no sign of a struggle in the car where I found Artie and Ms. Sykes. So, he must have been easy pickings for whoever shot him. Artie'd even opened the window for them. Did he know them, or had someone acted as if they needed help and got him to roll the window down?

The whole Kerabolt question kept popping up, also. Assuming he was using it without FDA approval, where was he getting it, and how did he get it past the other partners? Unless Bobby, Malcolm, and Rachel were also involved. Rachel seemed so distraught, so out of her element, when the police came, it made me want to rule her out. I could more easily believe Malcolm was involved. He was a good guy, but I always thought easily influenced by Artie. Bobby made that comment about Artie putting them all in jeopardy. I'd known Bobby the longest. Maybe I'd go talk to him. It was hard to believe he'd been involved in anything illegal, but I would press him to explain the comment he made the other day.

"Chicken done yet?" Lynn's voice behind me made me jump.

"Yeah, sorry. I was just thinking about Artie again. What he was hiding."

"It was probably that he was using that Kerabolt illegally, like you said. If he had been using it as part of a study, why would he hide it?"

"I agree. He always did believe he was right. If he believed the hype and thought it would truly benefit his patients, I can see him using it with or without FDA approval." I didn't add that his motive was just as likely financial.

"What would happen to him if he got caught?" Lynn asked.

I put the plate of chicken on the picnic table. "That's what doesn't make a lot of sense to me. I think he, well, the group itself probably, would get fined. While that would be bad, it doesn't seem like it would make someone want to kill him."

"Unless it wasn't the first time they'd been fined for unethical practices," Lynn said.

"Then the penalty would be stiffer, maybe even loss of license. If that's true, that means that someone in High Life Derm did have motive to kill Artie." I considered this for a moment, and then shook my head. "No, I've known his partners for years. I wouldn't blame them if they refused to cover for him and let him take the fall for what he's done, but I can't see any of them killing him."

Lynn stood up. "If the other doctors were involved, an investigation would put extra stress on them. As I said, you never know what a person will do under stressful circumstances. Plus, don't forget, it looks like Artie was about to ditch whoever his partners in crime were."

That was true, and again it shifted blame somewhere I didn't want to go. "That doesn't tell us either why I'm still involved, or what it is someone thinks I have." The chicken was getting cold, and while I didn't have much of an appetite anymore, I hated to see the food go to waste. "Let's eat out here."

"Sure. I'll bring out the salad and rolls."

I watched Lynn stride back into the house. I thought about how much I didn't know about her. I had begun to feel like we'd known each other for ages instead of only a few weeks. But it still all went back to Artie being the link, and it turned out there was a lot about Artie I never knew, either.

We ate in silence. I kept taking covert glances at Lynn. Our eyes met finally, and I realized she had been doing the same thing to me. We both smiled, embarrassed.

Lynn cleared her throat and said, "I'm sorry, Melanie. I haven't told you the whole truth. About Artie, I mean. I said I hadn't had any contact with him in years. It was really no big deal, but I wrote him when Doug and I first started having problems. Just a 'Hey, how are you, how are things going?' kind of letter. I told him I had been thinking about him and remembering our early days together." She looked away, toward the marsh across the street. "I guess I just wanted to be reassured he still had some good memories of our marriage. He never answered my letter, which may be a good thing. I mean, he had married twice since he was married to me. I didn't really want to start anything up again, and it might have proved awkward if he had written back. But you can imagine how I felt when I found out he never even mentioned to you having been married to me."

She swallowed, and I could see tears had welled up in her eyes. I reached out to put my hand on her arm.

"Anyway." She looked at me. "I really do have an old college roommate who lives here in Connecticut, and that is how I heard about Artie's death. But that day, when you found me trying to get into his office, I wasn't just looking to see if Artie still had the painting I did for him. I wanted to see if he kept my letter."

"But it wasn't there, was it?" I said.

"No." Her voice was soft.

I felt awkward saying it, but "It's probably just as well. I mean, is it something the police might—"

"Oh, no. There was nothing in it that was likely to make me a suspect. I sent it over a year ago." She pushed her food around on her plate for a few seconds, "But...he could have at least texted or sent a brief note in reply."

I poured her a glass of lemonade and refilled my own glass. "To Artie—King of the Jerks!" We clinked glasses.

Chapter Sixteen

I slept poorly again that night. I kept turning over in my mind the possibility that someone in Artie's office was involved in his murder. I really didn't think it possible, but Lynn had made a good point in saying that you never really could say how people would react when under extreme stress. I think losing your livelihood and your professional license would qualify as extreme stress.

I decided to visit Bobby the next day after work. I could see if "Kerabolt" had any meaning to him, and maybe just reassure myself that the idea any of Artie's colleagues would be involved in murder was ridiculous. I didn't call before I went to his house. I figured the best chance of getting information out of him, and to gauge his reaction, was to catch him off guard.

Bobby answered the door dressed in a tux. Not the after-work attire I'd expected. "Hi. I was wondering if I could come in for just a minute. I wanted to ask you a couple of quick questions."

Bobby looked at his watch and stepped away from the door to let me in. "I'm running late. I'm supposed to be at the New Haven County Medical Association dinner. Susan is meeting me there. I can give you about thirty seconds, then I have to go."

I stepped into the living room to my left and took a seat on the loveseat. Bobby stood near the doorway, taking out his phone as if to check for messages or calls.

I cleared my throat, "I'd like to know what information you have on the drug Kerabolt, and if Artie was using it to treat his patients."

Bobby's eyes did a quick flicker of either surprise or guilt; I wasn't sure which. "Kerabolt? Where'd you hear about that?"

"It was in some papers I found when I took Artie's things from his office." Not a complete lie, I was able to deduce the drug name from the few letters on the forms I'd found.

He said a few obscenities under his breath. "Look, I don't know what you read, or what was in those papers, but leave the whole issue alone. Please."

I felt my temper flare briefly, "Everyone keeps telling me to leave it alone, but my house was broken into and my dog terrorized by someone apparently looking for something they thought I had. Malcolm tried to warn me to get rid of 'it' but won't say what, and Renata called to speak to me about something, then she's killed before she can tell me what it was. I would love to leave things alone, but I'm getting a little nervous, to say the least. I would like things wrapped up before anything else happens."

"What makes you think it has to do with this drug?"

I shook my head, "I don't know for sure, but it's a place to start, and so far, everyone seems to tense up when I ask about it."

Bobby took a deep breath, "Okay. What do you know about Kerabolt?"

"Only what I've been able to get off the internet. That although it was developed to treat certain skin conditions, it's become the next "big thing" in age reversal. That patients don't have to get injections. It can be given orally. And that it's not yet approved by the FDA for use in this country."

Bobby nodded and looked at his watch again. "Like I said, I only have a few minutes, so I'll cut to the chase. Forget what you read about Kerabolt and its wonder powers. Yeah, some people say they saw an effect within a couple of months, but little is known about how long the effects last. More importantly, there can be dangerous side effects. Data shows that 30% of patients who used the drug in the studies in this country developed abnormal liver function tests within six months, and there was a threefold increase in liver and colon cancers among those using it. It's poison. I told Artie that, said we should not under any circumstances be using it with our patients. He pooh-poohed the reports of side effects, said there were other factors present in those study patients who trialed the drug and developed tumors or abnormal lab results. He showed me the research protocol he'd obtained;

he said we'd make a bundle if we got in on the ground floor. Turns out the research protocol was a fake, forged."

If what he said about the side effects was true, this was an even bigger mess than I first thought. "How did you find out about the research protocol being forged?"

"The police said so, when they brought me in for questioning after Artie was killed."

Bobby had taken a seat on the arm of the sofa opposite me, he seemed to have forgotten about the time, and I was not about to remind him.

"Do you really think Artie was using Kerabolt on his patients?"

Bobby rubbed his cheeks with his hands and nodded. "Yeah, I was pretty sure at the time, but I hid behind the 'don't ask' policy, because I didn't know what I would do if the answer was yes. Now, of course, I'm sure he was. The cops didn't come right out and say it, but from what I was able to pick up, the FDA was investigating our practice at the time Artie was killed. They had gotten wind of Artie's fabricated protocol and were gathering evidence to close in. I'm not sure what will happen now."

The look on Bobby's face made me feel sorry for him, but what he said had done nothing to allay my fears about who might have killed Artie and Ms. Sykes. "But you weren't involved, right? How about the other partners?"

"If I believe Malcolm, he says he didn't participate in the "trial," but the other night, he admitted that he knew Artie was."

"And Rachel?"

He snorted and shook his head. "No, I don't know. Even before Artie was killed, it was like she was hardly ever there anymore, if you know what I mean."

"Not exactly, no."

"When she is there at the office, she is not really THERE. She sees a few patients, then leaves. She's got her own problems, something personal."

"Do you know what it is?"

Bobby shook his head, "Someone in her family is ill, I think. I guess it's insensitive to admit this, but I never asked. Rachel is very private about her personal life, and I never pressed her to find out what was going on. I told myself I was giving her her space."

"Would Artie have known what was going on?" I asked.

"Probably. You know how he was, Mr. Charm and Personality. He made it his business to know everything that was going on. Anyway, things have been a little strained in the office the last few months."

It looked like even before Artie's death something was making the practice implode. "Just one more question, do you have any idea where Artie was getting the drug, or who helped him get the fake research verification?"

"Don't you think if I did, I'd go to the police with it?" He got up suddenly, "Look, I have to go. Sorry, but I've told you all I really know, and I'm not about to make any conjectures. I don't know if any of this has anything to do with whoever thinks you have something they want. I hope not, because it's a mess, believe me." He escorted me to the door, and as he opened it, he said, "Just let the police do their work, don't get more involved. I don't want to see you get hurt too. Let Artie go."

I turned as I was about to leave, "What about the Sykes woman? Malcolm says she was providing fake I.D. for him to escape before the Feds closed in. Is that true?"

Bobby shook his head, "I don't know. But that does sound like Artie, doesn't it?"

I left not feeling any better about the lack of motive for one of the partners to want Artie "gone." But I knew Bobby and Malcolm, and while they might leave Artie holding the bag for what he'd done, as he should have been, they would never harm him. While I didn't know Rachel as well, she just seemed too mild tempered to ever physically hurt a person.

It was obvious both Bobby and Tori's sister, Zeta, didn't think much of Kerabolt. What I didn't know was if it had anything to do with why Artie was killed, or if it was connected to what someone wanted from me.

Chapter Seventeen

The next day didn't offer much chance to obsess over whether one of Artie's former partners was involved in his murder, or over the fact that Bruno was going bald, or even that my ex-husband's first wife was now my roommate, and how strange that was. It seemed every patient visit I made offered a complication or a misstep on someone's part. I found Mrs. Waters feverish and confused, and far too many of her antibiotics left in the prescription bottle. Winnie Fried DID NOT LIKE the skinny little aide the agency sent to help her bathe, according to Winnie the woman spoke in entirely too soft a voice to be picked up clearly by Winnie's hearing aid, and "she hovers over me too much, I'm not as unsteady as I look!" The blood pressure meds Edgar Mott had picked up from the pharmacy were the wrong dose, and it required several calls to the pharmacy and his physician's office to sort out the problem. At five PM I finally got a chance to call the vet's office and speak to Dr. Reddy. He prescribed a stronger cortisone/antibiotic cream for Bruno's bare patches and told me to continue with the behavioral training Dr. McKenzie had me doing with Bruno. I sighed. Maybe *this* cream would work. At least Bruno seemed to be having fewer accidents and had stopped peeing in inappropriate places.

I passed two bicyclists on my way home and decided what I needed was exercise: a long walk near the beach with Bruno, just the two of us. Maybe I could clear my mind, forget all about the whole mess surrounding Artie's murder. I also remembered Justin MacKenzie's words that my stress would transfer to Bruno, so I would be doing both of us a service by unwinding at the beach. The rumbling in my stomach reminded me that I hadn't eaten anything since a yogurt at 11 AM. I had to admit that Lynn had been great about making dinner on the days I'd worked, and despite her comment about sleeping with Artie again if he hadn't been killed, we did seem to get along well.

I found Lynn seated at the kitchen table, two places set, and the smell of chili in the air. She had a smug look on her face. "Hi, how was your day?"

I sighed and plopped down my laptop bag and work bag on a chair. "Long. What's going on?" I bent to scratch under Bruno's chin as he sniffed around my feet. I looked up again as Lynn cleared her throat.

"I was just thinking that I never told you much about the time when Artie and I were first married."

"Is this something I'm really going to want to hear, because I'm starving, and I wouldn't want my appetite ruined."

She laughed. "No, nothing like that. I told you I supported Artie while he was in medical school. Well, I worked as a receptionist in an optometrist's office."

I got up and grabbed our bowls and brought them to the stove, and started to fill them. "Yes, so?"

"So, not to sound callous, but as I mentioned before, I need a job. Highlife Dermatology needs a receptionist since Renata was killed and Kaylee Hogarth left the receptionist position and replaced her as Office Manager."

I took a bite of chili—delicious. "I thought her name was Kiley." The ramifications of what she suggested suddenly hit me. "Holy mackerel, that would be great, but do you really think they would hire you?"

"Oh, but they did. I had an interview this afternoon, and Ms. Kaylee Hogarth offered me the job. Part-time, but it will be a steady paycheck. I can pay you rent, and I can keep track of what is going on in the office."

I stared at her. "That is a good idea. Actually, it's a great idea!" I ate a little more of the chili. "Wait a minute, though. Didn't Malcolm or Bobby recognize you?"

"Why would they object to my working there, unless there was something to hide? They weren't there today anyway, at least not while I was there. Ms.

Hogarth introduced me to Rachel Hayward, but she didn't seem to recognize me, and in fact, barely paid any attention to me at all. I applied as Lynn Duncan. I legally dropped the Krapaneck after the divorce from Artie."

"They will make you sign a confidentiality agreement."

"Already did. But that applies to patients, not to staff behaving illegally or unprofessionally."

"When do you start work?" I broke off a small piece of crusty bread and offered it to Bruno under the table.

"I start orientation tomorrow at eight AM. Also, Ms. Hogarth mentioned that the physician they hired to fill Artie's spot is starting tomorrow. It should be an interesting day."

It was weird to think of someone else in the office that Artie had occupied since the practice started, but of course, it was inevitable. "I spoke to Bobby yesterday. There definitely was some illegal activity going on before Artie was killed. He admitted it was linked to this Kerabolt, but said they are under scrutiny by the FDA, so I don't know if anything is still going on. Also, he seems to think Artie was the only one involved."

"That could be, but I still need a job, and this way, we can find out if he's telling the truth." Lynn wiped the last of the chili from her bowl with a slice of bread. "Do you believe what he said?"

I cleared our bowls, rinsed them, and put them in the dishwasher. I hated the thought of Bobby not being totally honest with me, but I still felt like he was holding something back. "No, not all of it, so be careful. There have been a lot of mishaps connected to that place lately."

"I will. Did I also fail to mention that I am versed in Krav Maga? I started training anyway, back when Artie and I were together, and I had a lot of lonely nights while he was on call. I may be a little rusty, but I remember some of it, and I bet I could do some damage if accosted."

More I didn't know or suspect about Lynn. "Well, good. But isn't defusing conflict part of Krav Maga? Better to focus on that."

She nodded. "Don't worry. I pride myself on my ability to avoid conflict."

Lynn said she had to pick out something appropriate to wear on her first day at the office, which helped avoid the necessity of inviting her along on my walk. So, although the sun would be setting soon, I grabbed Bruno's leash.

I was not the only one who thought an evening walk or ride along the beach would be a good idea. Two other cars pulled into a lot a quarter full at Hammonnassett Beach State Park. A couple in their twenties with two small children and a guy who was taking a bike from a rack on the back of his SUV all arrived as Bruno and I did. Dogs were forbidden on the beach itself, so I made my way to the bike path and started out at a brisk pace. Bruno pranced along as we made our way on the sand and gravel path. Bruno stopped to sniff a spot as a rabbit hopped into the seagrass and beach roses lining the path, and I paused to watch the sun as it began to sink from a mauve and lavender sky into the ocean. Any day that ended with a sight like this couldn't be counted as all bad.

I felt, as well as heard, the soft gravel crunch of a bike approaching behind me, and if I'd hesitated another three seconds, I would have found myself flung up onto the handlebars. I dove into the beach roses along the path and felt the jerk of Bruno's leash as it must have snagged on part of the bike. I had the leash wrapped on my wrist, and the fact that it had a break-away attachment to his collar saved Bruno from being whisked away as the rider wobbled on, then regained his balance and took off without even looking back.

"Holy Cow! What a jerk!" A small thin woman who looked to be in her fifties had come over to stand above me. "Let me help you up."

"Thanks," I said as she guided me to my feet.

"Heavens, are you badly hurt?" Another woman was standing with the first.

I brushed sand from my knees and bent to examine Bruno for injuries. He licked my face as I ran my hands over him, and determined he was no worse for the incident. I didn't fare as well. The thorns on the beach rose bushes had left scratches all up my arms, and I felt a stinging on my right cheek. "Only slightly injured. I think."

The woman who had helped me up now stood with her hands on her hips, looking down the path in the direction the bicyclist had disappeared. "He didn't even stop. At least, I think it was a he. Can't tell with all these biking clothes they wear."

Her companion, another woman in her fifties or sixties offered me a tissue and motioned at my face. "It was a man, all right. He came tearing around us and swerved right toward you. I couldn't see his face. He had on a red bicycle racing helmet. Good thing too, since he obviously is a maniac, and a rude one at that!"

The first woman shook her head, "No, I think his helmet was orange, with a black stripe."

"No, Sarah, I'm sure it was red, but maybe it did have a racing stripe now that you mention it."

The tissue the Good Samaritan gave me to wipe my face came away with blood, and my hands were shaking so badly I could hardly get Bruno's leash undone from my wrist. "It was good of you to stop to help. I think I'll be all right now." I snapped Bruno's leash back on his collar and secured it on my wrist again.

"Well, if you want to walk a while with us, you're welcome."

All the calm I had claimed a minute before was gone, "Thank you, but I think Bruno and I are done for tonight. The park will be closing soon anyway."

"All right, take care, dear." They waved as they continued on the path.

I looked behind me every few minutes on the way back to the car; I kept feeling as if someone was following me. I tried to dispel the feeling. The incident was probably just some hot shot on a racing bike. But no matter what my rational mind told me, my gut told me that there had been a purpose to that guy nearly plastering me on the bike path. I didn't know if I actually saw or only imagined his hand shooting out as he passed me. What would he have wanted with me, anyway? And who would even know I was going to be at this particular beach at this time? I thought back to the other people who had arrived in the parking lot the same time as I did. There had been a cyclist. I noticed him taking his bike down from the rack on his SUV. His vehicle was blue, but I couldn't remember or never noticed the make of it. There were two blue SUVs in the lot when I returned, both parked nearly next to each other. Both had bike racks fastened to their backs and no driver in sight. The only thing I could remember about the man I saw when I came in was that he *was* a man, maybe not too old. Great, I thought, it was useless to even report the incident to the park rangers. All I had was a guy between teenage and geezer-hood who drove a blue vehicle of some kind. Also, I realized I was probably making a bigger deal out of it than it warranted. It seemed farfetched that I was followed, and other than sheer coincidence that was the only way the bicyclist would know I was here.

It was almost full dark in the few minutes it took to drive home. Lynn was in the kitchen, concentrating on ironing a cream-colored blouse as I walked in. Her usual outfit, as long as I had known her, had always been either a T-shirt and shorts or a long flowing cotton skirt and tank top.

"Hi. Are you going somewhere?"

"No. I thought I'd get my clothes ready for work tomorrow. I figured I could start out conservative and get a little more "me" as I'm there a bit longer." She glanced up and gasped, "What happened to you? You look like you were mugged!"

"I sort of was." I told her about the guy on the bike path. "Anyway, it probably was just a spur-of-the-moment thing, maybe he mistook Bruno's leash for a purse strap, but it still makes me nervous. I've done home nursing visits in downtown New Haven and not had as many brushes with crime as I have in the past month."

Lynn shook her head, "Maybe it was a coincidence, but I don't blame you for being nervous."

The scratches on my arms and cheek had really started to sting, "I'm going to take a shower and put something on these scratches."

There was a knock on the front door as I passed from the kitchen toward the bedroom to gather my things.

I sighed with resignation as I opened the door.

The smile on Detective Cody's face was more cordial than sincere. "Good evening Ms. Bass. Could I come in for a moment?"

I stepped back to allow her to enter, my first thought being: "How did she know about the attempted mugging at Hamonassett Beach, and why would it be her problem? "Did someone call you about that crazy biker at the beach? Really, it was nothing I...."

The blank look on her face stopped me from saying anything more.

"I'm sorry, I don't know what you're talking about. What biker?"

I rubbed the scratches on my arms. "It was just some guy on the bike path at Hammonassett. He brushed against me and sent me into the beach roses. It was really no big deal." I suddenly felt silly at the paranoia I'd felt a few minutes before. Detective Cody didn't say anything for a few minutes, but I saw her looking at the scratches on my arms and face.

"Did he say anything as he pushed you? Did you report the encounter to the ranger?"

"No, I didn't report it, but maybe I should have. I thought he might have been grabbing for what he took for my purse strap but was instead Bruno's leash. At the time, I just wanted to go home, and really there was no harm other than a few scratches."

She gave me a look that made me feel like I was the one in the wrong here. "Still, it seems as if the individual was intent on committing a crime, no matter the outcome. Next time contact the ranger."

Did she expect a next time? I was about to ask, but she cut me off with another question.

"The reason I stopped by was I need to ask you again if you have any information on any of Mr. Krapaneck's patients or if he discussed any of his work with you before he died."

"No, Artie would never discuss patients. That's against the law." I realized how silly that statement sounded in light of what I now knew about him, but the Artie I thought I knew would never do that. "Besides, as I told you earlier, we really only talked about the most mundane pleasantries or Bruno when we met to exchange his custody." I was getting downright irritated now. First, I was chastised for not reporting a crime when I was the victim, then it seemed as if she was questioning my honesty. I did have one quick guilty thought about what Bobby told me about Kerabolt, but I was pretty sure they knew as much as I did.

Detective Cody seemed as if she was choosing her words carefully. "I'm not sure if you have heard from any of his colleagues or co-workers that we are co-operating with certain agencies in investigating illegal activities Dr. Krapaneck is alleged to have been involved in prior to his death."

Lynn had come into the living room as we were talking, and started to say, "Do...", but I gave her what I hoped was a subtle nudge.

"I had heard rumors from some of his peers, but nothing specific. And you mentioned before that there were other agencies involved. But I don't know any more than that. What was he supposedly doing?" Playing innocent didn't constitute dishonesty, I figured, plus I wanted to hear it in her own words.

"I am not at liberty to say, but if you do have any information, some papers, for instance, you have not turned over to us, it might be in your best interests to do so now."

Wait, did she think I was involved with Kerabolt too? "What do you mean? Do you think I was involved somehow? I had nothing to do with any "illegal activities" he might have been involved in, and I'm not covering for him, either if you were implying that."

"Do we need to call a lawyer?" Lynn asked.

"No, you don't need to call a lawyer. All I was implying, at this point, is that if you have information about what specifically he was doing, and who he was doing it with, you need to hand it over to me now."

"I have nothing to give you." I had to fight to keep the anger out of my voice. "I gave you all of the papers I found in Artie's belongings when you came to collect them last week. I would gladly hand over any information if I had it."

She got up and brushed off the back of her pants as if to rid them of offending dog hairs. I refrained from my first impulse to tell her my dog doesn't shed.

She looked at me as if debating whether to say something or not, then, "It is likely Dr. Krapaneck left some very incriminating information about his former associates in crime somewhere. Given the pattern of break-ins and brushes with disaster you've had in the past weeks, maybe I'm not the only one who thinks you may have the information we need. Just be careful." She strode to the door and let herself out, closing the door firmly behind her.

Chapter Eighteen

Lynn and I sat up for several more hours. We re-hashed everything that had happened over the past two weeks but could not come up with anything to connect the dots. After I finally fell asleep, Bruno woke me up at 5 AM. He seemed restless and unable to settle down to sleep again. I took him out for a quick walk in the backyard, thinking he had to relieve himself. The sun had barely begun to rise, and a few birds had started their early morning chirping. Instead of relaxing in the morning peace, I tried to get rid of the pervading sense of anxiety I'd had since detective Cody had left the previous evening. Were her words meant as a threat or a warning? I found myself looking uncomfortably around the yard, at the small stand of trees and bushes that lined the other side of the backyard fence. My anxiety was quickly turning to anger that I had been made fearful on my own property and in my own house.

Bruno finished his business and began to tug on his leash, so we headed back inside. I was too keyed up to sleep again and sat in the living room to try to map out my next plan of action. Even if my sense of control was an illusion, it was what I needed to do. Bruno was curled up next to me on the sofa and began to chew at his right hip area again. I sighed and gently guided his head away from his chewing and tried to distract him. However, when I ran my hand over the area he had been gnawing at, I could feel a lump. Bruno let out a small "yip" and leapt up and limped away. There really was something wrong with his leg this time. My guess was that he had not come away as unhurt as I thought by our excursion into the beach rose bushes, he probably had a thorn that had embedded itself and had started to form an abscess. Worries about Artie's shady actions and how I was now involved were pushed aside. First order of business today would be to get Bruno seen by the vet.

It had begun to seem like I might as well have had the vet's office on speed dial for the number of times I'd had to call him in the past month. The voice that answered the phone did not belong to Traci, the regular receptionist at Dr. Reddy's office. "Sachem Veterinary office. This is Shawnee speaking."

"Hi, this is Melanie Bass, my dog Bruno is a patient of Dr. Reddy and Dr. McKenzie. He seems to be having trouble walking on his right rear leg this morning, and I can feel a lump near his right hip."

"Oh, dear. Can you give me your name again, please?"

I could hear the computer keys clicking after I told her.

"This is for Bruno? Doctor Reddy is off, and Doctor McKenzie is on today. He can see him at 10:00 if you could bring him in then." She sounded very young.

I did a mental calculation. It was 8:20 already; Lynn had left for work in order not to be late on her first day, and I had a 9 o'clock family meeting with the Peters family. Hattie Peters was progressing rapidly in her dementia, and Frank D'Oria, her physician, Alice Myers, the social worker with my agency, and I had arranged to meet with her family to discuss options. I couldn't make it to the meeting at Dr. D'Oria's office and back home to pick up Bruno in time to make it by 10:00. "Do you think I could drop him off now, and Doctor McKenzie could see him at 10:00? You could call and let me know when he is ready to be picked up. Traci and Doctor Reddy usually let me do that when I have a work appointment and can't reschedule."

She hesitated, but then, "Sure, Okay. If that's what you usually do. Like I said, Dr. Reddy isn't in the office today, it's Dr. McKenzie. He's new, but he seems nice. He probably won't mind if you drop him off."

Again, I was struck by how young she sounded, but I dismissed those thoughts quickly as I thought about seeing Justin again today. Poor Bruno, here he was not feeling well, and all I could think about was how pleased I was to have a reason to talk to his vet!

When I carried Bruno and his pet carrier in and connected the face to the voice, I realized "Shawnee" was even younger than she sounded on the phone. I thought she sounded to be in her early twenties, but she looked to be barely out of high school.

She snatched him out of my arms. "Oh, he's so cute! Come here, pretty baby. What's wrong? You have a boo-boo?" Bruno only wiggled a little when she put her hand under his sore hip.

"Traci is out today, I guess?"

"Yeah, some kind of family emergency, I think. I work for Timely Temps, but this is the best job they ever sent me on! When I graduate, I'm gonna go to college to be a vet." She made smooching noises at Bruno, and he looked mournfully in my direction. "Come on, little guy. I'll put you in back until the doctor can see you." She looked up at me. "Don't worry, I'll take good care of him."

I handed over Bruno's pet carrier, "You can put him in here if he needs to wait a few minutes for me. Will you call when he's ready? I have a meeting at nine AM, but I can come any time after I'm done, and please let the doctor know I want to talk to him when I pick up Bruno."

"Sure thing."

I was already tense at the thought that Mrs. Peter's son and daughter-in-law had resisted any change in her lifestyle up to this point, citing "Mother would never want to be in a 'rest home,' she'd just die!" I had found Mrs. Peters dehydrated and semi-conscious three days before, and even after receiving IV fluids in the hospital, she was unable to remember the last time she ate or drank anything. Now Shawnee and her seeming inexperience was giving me a whole new stressor. I tried to reassure myself Bruno would be fine; I'd go back to the vet and get him as soon as I was done with my meeting. It was lucky that Justin McKenzie was on, too. I'd been wanting to speak to him about how Bruno was doing anyway, and well, I blushed to admit to myself, I just wanted to speak with him in general.

The Peters proved to be even more resistant to the obvious choices for their mother than I'd expected. Moving in with them was out, they traveled extensively; 24-hour home health care was an option, but very costly. Alice convinced them that she had a very well rated facility in mind for their mother, not too far away, and while pricier than some, still less expensive than 24-hour home care. We all agreed, finally, with Alice's suggestion, but it took 2 hours, not the forty-five minutes to an hour I'd expected.

When I got back into the car, I checked my cell phone and found I had two messages. The first was from Lynn. "Hi, Mel. First let me say that the new derm guy is gorgeous, and single. But what I called to tell you was that there are cops all over the office now, they are trying to be discrete, but something is going on. I have to go. I'll get back to you when I find out what's happening."

Wow. It really was working out having Lynn "embedded" at High Life Derm. The second message was from the vet's office; Bruno was ready to be picked up. Poor Bruno, I hoped Shawnee had been true to her word and taken good care of him.

Shawnee greeted me with a smile but looked slightly confused as I approached the reception counter.

"Hi. I'm here to pick up Bruno. I'm sorry I'm late. My meeting ran longer than expected, and—"

Shawnee's smile froze. "But someone already picked Brutus up. About an hour ago."

"What! How? Who?"

"I called your cell phone and left a message, and tried your home phone, too. You didn't get back to me." I thought her color got suddenly paler.

"Who took Bruno?" My voice was louder than I'd intended. I tried to remind myself she was basically a child, and yelling never solved anything as I'd told all my disgruntled patients. Unfortunately, yelling seemed all I was capable of at that moment.

Shawnee's eyes filled with tears. "I tried the other number listed on Brutus's contact info. The lady that answered said she would come and get him. It was listed as an emergency contact, so I thought it was all right."

Artie's number. I'd never even thought to remove it after he died. "That number was no longer supposed to be used!" I was angry at my own stupidity and was taking it out on Shawnee.

My yelling brought two vet techs and Justin McKenzie from the treatment area in the back. Justin looked at me as if I had lost my mind. "Melanie, what's wrong? Bruno is fine. I removed a large thorn. He had a small abscess that must have come from an earlier injury. I washed that out and gave him a first dose of antibiotic. I also took some x-rays to be sure the bone wasn't involved, but I don't think that's likely. I had to give him a little anesthesia, but he did well. Just complete the antibiotic course, and he should be fine." He looked around for a moment, "Where is Bruno?"

"That's what I want to know." I explained to him what had happened.

Shawnee was crying full out now. "I didn't know! I'm sorry."

I took my voice down several notches to as close to soothing as I could muster at that moment. "What did the woman who took Bruno look like? Did she leave her name when she paid the bill or anything?" I knew who it must have been who came to get him, but it made no sense to me.

"She was tall, real chic cut black hair, and dressed in expensive clothes. She didn't pay. She said put it on your account. That's how you usually did it when she picked up Brutus."

"Bruno! His name is Bruno." I was shouting again, and poor Shawnee flinched.

"She said she was glad to do you a favor and get Bruno home, so he could rest."

There was something else that puzzled me. "He went to her? He didn't struggle?"

Shawnee shook her head. "No, she popped him right in the pet carrier. He was still kind of sleepy, though."

Justin looked a little pale now. He turned to me, "Who would have come to pick him up?"

"My ex-husband's number was still in your system. It was probably his widow, Tori, a woman who never could stand Bruno, and who has no right to take him." I could feel my face flushing with anger.

Justin reached for the phone on the desk. "I'm so sorry. This is unacceptable. I'll call the police right now—"

"No. Please. I'll take care of it. I have no idea why Tori would want to take

Bruno, but believe me, I plan to find out." I pulled two tissues from the box on the counter and handed them to Shawnee. "Here. I know you referred to Bruno's file, so I guess I'm to blame for not updating it." A woman with a meowling cat in a cat carrier had entered and stood aghast, watching the scene in front of her.

Justin said, "Please let me know when you have him back."

I just waved a dismissive hand at him and walked out the door. I didn't know why I was angry at him, but suddenly it just seemed like anger, no rage, at everyone and everything had just bubbled to the surface.

When my cell phone rang just as I was about to jam the car into drive, I answered it with a terse "Yes" without even checking the caller ID.

Lynn seemed not to even have noticed my abruptness. "It's me. You won't believe it. They're taking Rachel Harwood in for questioning. Something to do with her sister. Whatever it was, I heard she and Artie had a big fight, and she threatened Artie before he was killed." She was whispering.

"What? How was Artie involved with Rachel's sister? And why in the world would Rachel threaten him?"

"I don't know. I have to go. I'll let you know."

"I have to go too. They took Bruno."

"What? Who…?"

I punched the off button on the cell. Rachel arrested? Lynn was right, I couldn't believe it, but right now, my priority was getting Bruno back.

Chapter Nineteen

I tried to stay within the posted speed limit, my anger making even seventy miles an hour seem like a snail's pace. I had no idea why the hell Tori would pick up Bruno from the vet. At least I assumed it was her who took Bruno, although Shawnee said the woman who took him was stylishly dressed, and that certainly did not describe Tori the last time I saw her. I felt my anger building to an even more feverish pitch. How dare she! Bruno was practically my child, and Tori had no right to him, no matter what anyone said. I had changed my mind and called the police after leaving the Veterinarian's office, but they were no help. They explained that Tori was heir to Artie's estate, and since he'd had partial ownership of Bruno, the dog was part of that estate. I swerved around a Honda Civic doing a mere 65 in the passing lane. Justin McKenzie said he would notify the temp agency that the receptionist they sent screwed up. I told him not to, however. I still couldn't believe she handed over Bruno to Tori, but I had to admit it wasn't totally her fault.

I screeched off the highway onto the exit ramp and headed toward Tori's. There weren't any cars in the circular drive when I pulled up, and I assumed her car was in the garage. I stopped at the end of the portico that led to the front door, and I jumped out. I poked the doorbell three times in quick succession, ready to firmly tell Elaina that I didn't care what Mrs. Krapaneck was doing at the moment. I wanted a word with her. I secretly hoped Bruno would rush out around Elaina's feet and I would be spared any attempt at civility with Tori. I hit the bell rapid fire several times again. No response. I had never even considered that Tori would not be home. Damn it, where was Elaina and where did Tori have my dog! I decided to look around the property; maybe she had taken Bruno for a walk; that she might truly be taking good care of him was a fleeting but comforting thought. Then just as rapidly, I got a sick feeling in my stomach, and scenes from 101 Dalmatians, Cruella DeVille in her spotted dog hide jacket, played over in my head.

"Hello! Tori! Come, Bruno, come on, boy!" I yelled as I made a canvas of the property. I thought that once I heard voices and a muffled little bark, but then again, I might have imagined it. There was no one in sight, and no one answered my calls. Damn! I went up to the front door again and jiggled the knob in frustration. I was caught off balance as the door swung open. I edged into the entryway. I had rung the bell, I had called out, so I didn't think it was breaking and entering, and besides, I didn't really care. I wanted Bruno back, and then I would leave. "Bruno! Here boy!" My voice was a stage whisper, but there were no other sounds from anywhere in the house. I called louder, "Bruno! Mommy's here, come on, fella." No joyous barking, no skittering of little feet. I did, however, hear a loud thump from upstairs. I took the stairs two at a time, not sure who was up there but determined that they hand over Bruno.

The first room on the right looked to be a guest bedroom when I opened the door. It was empty. The next door on the right led to a palatial sized master bedroom. The drapes were pulled nearly closed, a single stream of sunlight leaking from one side of the window. The room smelled sour, and it felt stuffy as if the air conditioning was turned down. The king-size bed was rumpled, the sheets hanging off the far side of the bed. I started toward the window to open the drapes in order to get a better look, and from the corner of my eye I saw a crumpled form on the floor. Tori was lying on her back. Her eyes were half opened; her cheek was smeared with vomit, and, as I watched, one shuddering breath caused her chest to rise.

"Oh, God! Tori!" I rushed over to kneel next to her and shook her shoulder, trying to get a response. From downstairs, I heard a single, very familiar yelp, then the slamming of the front door.

Someone was leaving with Bruno, but Tori was simultaneously trying to check out before my very eyes. For one fleeting moment, I thought of leaving

Tori, and go tearing after Bruno and his captor, but knew I needed to give Tori my attention. I turned her onto her side and used the corner of the sheet to swipe out her mouth. She seemed to be making no further effort to breathe, so I flipped her onto her back and gave her two rescue breaths and prayed she'd get the hint and keep breathing on her own. One more heaving breath, then nothing. "Damn it, Tori, breathe!" I gave her another cycle of two breaths and checked for a pulse. What I felt was slow and weak, but her heart was at least still beating. I gave her another two breaths, then looked on the nightstand for the phone, relieved that they still had a landline.

"911, what is your emergency?"

"I'm at 1871 Chickadee Lane. I found…my friend…not breathing. I need an ambulance."

"I want you to—"

"Yes, I've already started rescue breathing. I have medical training. Please have them hurry. Someone's also stolen my dog, and I need to get him back." I realized how bizarre that second part must have sounded, but to me, it was very important information. "I'm with the woman in the upstairs bedroom." I could only identify her as my friend once in a day.

Tori had started to take a few more regular breaths while I spoke to the 911 operator, but still seemed to be unconscious. I pulled up an eyelid to reveal a pinpoint pupil. It looked like she had taken an overdose of whatever she had been on the day I last saw her. I shook her some more. "Tori! Wake up! Where is Bruno? Who was here with you?" Nothing. A long pause in her respirations, then another deep breath. I ran into the master bathroom for a cold wet cloth to wipe her face to try to get some reaction. I sponged off her face and neck and she let out a weak moan. I was relieved to hear the sound of sirens turning into the drive, quickly followed by the sound of heavy footsteps running up the stairs.

"Hello! Paramedics! Who needs help?"

"In here." I scrubbed Tori's face once again with the wet cloth, and her eyes opened a bit more. "Tori, where's Bruno?"

She opened her eyes wider for a moment and whispered something like "don't…" then reverted to limp and barely breathing.

"Okay, let me in, miss." One of the paramedics shouldered me aside and began to take Tori's vital signs and slap an oxygen mask on her, while another snagged her arm to start an IV.

There was a police officer standing on the other side of the bed from where Tori lay. "You the one called this in?"

"Yes. I came here to pick up my dog, and I found Tori unconscious on the floor."

He took a small pad and pen from his breast pocket. "What is the victim's name?"

"Victoria Krapaneck."

"She have any medical conditions that you know of?"

"No. I don't know, I mean. I do know she has been taking some kind of sedative recently due to the death of her husband." So very much information was missing from that brief explanation, but it seemed concise was called for at the moment. The paramedics had hoisted Tori onto a gurney and were wheeling her out by this time.

"How'd Mrs. Krapaneck seem since her husband's death? Was she overly distraught, mention any thoughts of suicide or hurting herself?"

"I don't know, her sister was staying with her for a while, she might know."

He looked around the room, "So where is this sister?"

"I don't know."

His look made it plain that he felt my pool of information was pretty shallow indeed. "Anyone else with her when you got here?"

"Nobody I could see, but when I went to help Tori, I heard someone leave, they had my dog Bruno with them. I could hear him yelping." I felt the sting of tears starting to form. "I want to report him as stolen, please."

I must have looked totally distraught because he nodded and flipped over to a new page, "Okay. What kind of dog, what does he look like?"

"He's about twelve pounds, a terrier mix, white and grey long-haired coat."

"I'll report it. Anyone you can think of who would be here with Mrs. Krapaneck who would take your dog?"

"No." I stifled a sob.

"Okay. We'll be on the lookout."

I nodded. "Can I leave now? I need to go look for Bruno."

"You can leave, but first, I need to get your name and number in case we have any more questions, or, you know, if we find your dog." After I gave him my information, he handed me a card with his name and contact information. "My name is Cooper. If you don't hear from me in a day or so, you can call the station. Ask for me." I barely looked at it and shoved it in my pocket.

The "if we find your dog" he'd said made my stomach lurch.

Chapter Twenty

I felt numb as I got behind the wheel of my car. I tried to tamp down the panic building in my chest. I didn't even know where to begin to look for Bruno, and the why questions kept playing over in my mind. Why would someone dognap Bruno? Why would Tori take a near fatal dose of sedatives, and was it possible that she had not intentionally overdosed? That thought added to the panic I felt. I was pulling out of the circular drive ahead of the police cruiser when I was startled by the sound of my cell phone. It was Justin McKenzie's office according to my caller ID.

"Hi, Melanie. I called to see if you got Bruno back."

"No." I began to sob. I pulled the car over, unable to talk, or even to see where I was going. Officer Cooper pulled up next to me and rolled down his window. I just waved him on.

"Are you alone now? Just take a deep breath." Justin's voice was calm but firm. "You need to call the police; you can't try to find him on your own."

"The police already know. I made a report." I started to regain control of myself, and I wiped my nose on a Dunkin Donuts napkin I found stuffed between the front seat and the center console. "I found Tori semi-comatose on sedatives. I heard Bruno bark, but then while I was with Tori calling for help, someone took off god knows where with him." I took several deep breaths as Justin had suggested, and I felt the jitters that had followed my crying jag start to recede.

Justin cleared his throat. "The reason I called, besides to make sure you had gotten Bruno back, was to tell you that I saw something I hadn't noticed before when I reviewed his x-rays."

"You mean he's sick, as well as missing?" I never cry, but here it was again. "You don't think it's—"

"No, I don't think he's sick. But I don't know what it is. I took a series of X-rays, just to make sure he didn't have any other sites of infection in his bones. I noticed a shadow between his shoulder blades, right where his ID chip is, but this is bigger than his ID chip."

"What is it, then?"

I heard him punching keys on his computer as if to bring up the x-ray on file. "It looks like a micro-chip, but different than the one that's supposed to be there."

"What do you mean? Could it possibly be another abscess? One that formed around his ID chip?"

"There's no fluid accumulated around it; it doesn't appear to be an abscess. It's definitely some type of hardware, but it's different than the kind of I.D. chip we would have used. Has Bruno had any surgeries done by another vet? Maybe your ex-husband had him treated somewhere else."

"I've always been the one who took Bruno to the vet. Artie didn't...." Suddenly I remembered that at the end of May, Artie had brought Bruno back from his "visitation" with a scab the size of a pencil eraser on the back of his neck. He had explained it as a scratch Bruno got from squeezing under the chicken wire fence surrounding the garden. He said the dog had been chasing a rabbit. "Justin, I'll need to call you back." I touched the end screen. Suddenly any urge to cry evaporated in the heat of the rage I felt. Artie. As a physician, he certainly had the means and the ability to do a little minor surgery on Bruno, maybe hide something he didn't want found. "That bastard!" This, of all the betrayals Artie had subjected me to, was the one that hurt me the most. No matter why he wanted the information hidden, I felt sick that he would put Bruno in a dangerous position. He had loved him almost as much as I did, or so I thought.

Tori, or whoever it was, who took Bruno from the veterinarian's office, was looking less and less like someone acting out of spite or on a weird whim. She was after something. But if it had been Tori, what happened to her after she got home? How did she get drugged to the point of unconsciousness?

Most importantly, who had Bruno now, and did they take him for leverage to get what they want, or did they know about the extra microchip?

I tried to calm myself, so I could think. I could tell by Officer Cooper's response that finding Bruno was not going to be a priority. I'd seen him look askance as I'd babbled about the theft of Bruno. One more lost dog was not going to rate an APB. But, I realized, if Detective Cody knew that Bruno might factor into the information they were looking for, she could get them to jump him up on the priority list. I just had to get her to believe my theory about Bruno having a microchip embedded in him that contained incriminating evidence against someone. I felt the cold fear grip my midsection again. There was no way to know how much time I had before whoever took him tried to recover that information. I didn't even want to think about how they would do it.

My hands shook as I fumbled in my purse for the card Sunny Cody had given me the other night. It was going to take me a lot longer to find Bruno on my own than if I had the help of the Police Department. She'd said it herself the other evening, there was an awful lot of coincidences in the bad luck I'd had lately. I was sure that she would agree that Bruno could be the link. If so, she would do all she could to find him. I punched in the number on her card but got a voicemail message to call 911 if this was an emergency or leave a message, and Detective Cody would get back to me as soon as possible. I felt the tears sting again. Where were the police when you needed them?

My voice shook as I left a message on Detective Cody's phone. "This is Melanie Bass. You asked me to call if I found out anything that related to my ex-husband Artie Krapaneck's activities before he was killed. I think I know where the information is, but we have to act fast. Please call me as soon as you get this."

I put my phone on the seat next to me, unsure where to go next. It began to ring almost immediately after I set it down. Cody. Thank God. But when I picked it up, it said, "number not found."

"Yes."

The voice was raspy, mechanical sounding. "We have the dog. Expect a call in half an hour, and you better have what we're looking for. Wait for instructions where to bring it. Refuse to co-operate, and I'll tell you where to find the dog's body. No cops." Then silence.

"Wait! I really don't know…." It was useless. The call was disconnected. I slowly set the phone down again. I felt both relief that whoever had Bruno had contacted me and horror that they really meant to harm him unless I gave them what they wanted. Then it hit me how ridiculous the situation was: either I was wrong and there was no microchip containing information embedded in Bruno, or they didn't realize they already had the information in their hands. I prayed it was the last option. I was reasonably sure they wouldn't take him to a nice clean vet's office to recover it. This thought made me shudder. I could try to make up an information source, and hope they fell for it long enough for me to grab Bruno and get away. Assuming they didn't know specifically what they were looking for. Where the hell was Cody? I needed someone who knew something about hostage negotiation from more than reading several hundred thriller novels. I placed my cell phone in my purse and decided to go home. It had been seven minutes since the dog nappers called, and I had no idea what to tell them when they called back. I had only a short time to come up with some sort of plan.

I began to pace back and forth in the kitchen as soon as I got home. Damn that poor Shawnee, if only she hadn't released Bruno to Tori. I stopped pacing as a thought occurred to me. She said Bruno was picked up by a tall dark-haired woman who wore nice clothes. I'd assumed it was Tori, but Tori had not been looking so put together lately, and when I found her, she certainly hadn't been wearing designer clothes. Zeta looks quite a bit like Tori. I had mistaken her for Tori myself. The day she came to my house to retrieve Artie's possessions, when I viewed her from the back, I thought it was Tori standing there. Another thought occurred to me, Zeta works for a pharmaceutical company. She'd dismissed Kerabolt as a sham when I questioned her, but her reaction seemed out of proportion for my having simply asked about the drug. Maybe she was covering up her own involvement in the Kerabolt deal and trying to get me off the track. It was hard to tell if the person who called me was a man or a deep voiced woman like Zeta. They had said "we." If Zeta was involved, then someone else must be working with her. That thought paralyzed me for a moment. If it was just her, I thought I might have a chance of getting away with Bruno. But if there were several of them I had no idea what to do.

I looked at the kitchen clock. I had fifteen minutes until they promised to call back. I grabbed a pen and paper from my purse. I had to think of something to tell them to stall or distract them when they called back. I had grabbed the pen Artie had given me as an anniversary present. I whispered, "Dammit, Artie, this is all because of you!" But I had no more time for anger or recriminations. I began to twist the barrel of the pen back and forth, my mind a blank. I took a deep breath. What was something Artie would have kept a record of that someone would want? Names? What names? Maybe I could make up a fake name, tell them Artie gave the item they wanted to them! The pen I had been twisting fell apart in my hands. Attached to one end was a flash drive.

I sat and stared at it for a couple of seconds. No need to make something up. It was possible Bruno's extra chip had nothing to do with what the dog nappers wanted. This could be it. I felt a slight release of the knot in my stomach. I started toward the desk where I kept my laptop.

It could just be a blank flash drive, just something Artie thought was cute. Or maybe he had recorded a message meant to smooth over one of his transgressions. I had no idea why he would get me something like this, anyway. There was only one way to find out. My nerves were stretched tight, waiting for Bruno's captors to call back. This was a small diversion, at least. Even if it was blank, I could write something on it that looked like information. Lord knew I'd heard enough of Artie's double speak explanations to fake something he might say. I paced back and forth, waiting for my laptop to boot up, each step marking seconds ticking by.

It wasn't blank after all. Nor was it a loving or fond message. Since I had thrown his gift at him, he must have decided to use it himself. The first thing to come up was two words: "Golden Goose" then a series of dates and numbers popped up on the screen. I'd seen that name, or at least the notation G. Goose, in the things I'd taken from Artie's office. I stared at the numbers, not knowing what they meant. Then I realized they must be dates and dollar amounts: "4/9- 10K, 4/13- 60K(!), 5/1- 23K." They seemed like huge amounts to be office expenditures. Maybe they reflected Artie's savings account. If so, he was far better off than I ever thought, the creep. Though this was a weird place to keep banking information. I did a quick guesstimate. The numbers and dates covered about two years, and I stopped when I got to three million dollars. Was the Golden Goose Kerabolt? If so, no wonder he was using it, legally or illegally. I tried to think of what else or who else the Golden Goose could be but could not think of anything. I continued to scroll down on the screen but jumped when my cell phone began to ring.

I had to take a few deep breaths again to calm my heart rate and breathing before I answered. The voice on the other end was distorted again, but not the same voice as had called the first time. "Rest stop between exits 61 and 62. Ten minutes. Go to the rear."

I had no time to come up with something else to hand over to them. I had no doubt that they meant it about harming Bruno if I didn't show up. I tucked the pen with the flash drive into the pocket of my shorts and grabbed my phone and purse. Nine minutes left to get there.

Chapter Twenty-One

My cell phone rang yet again as I was preparing to leave. It was Justin calling back. I was tempted to let it go to voice mail but thought maybe he had another suggestion about what he had seen on Bruno's x-ray. "Hello?"

"Melanie, it's Justin. I'm sorry I got you so worried about that shadow on Bruno's x-ray. I'm sure he'll be returned to you soon, and I just want you to bring him back in to be checked—"

I was rushing toward the car, seven minutes until I was supposed to meet the dog nappers. "I will bring him in, but first, I have to get him back. I might know where he is. I have to go."

"Go where? Where are you headed?"

"No time. I have to be at the rest stop between exit 61 and 62 in less than seven minutes." I pulled onto route 1. I prayed Public Works had finished the tree trimming they were doing earlier in the day. "Look, I'm driving, so I have to hang up."

"At the rest stop? I'll meet you there. You shouldn't go alone."

"No. They said not to bring anyone. Please. I'll be fine." I cut the connection before he could argue with me anymore. I felt the knot in my stomach tighten at the thought of going to the same rest stop where I'd found Artie's dead body. I focused instead on Bruno and how scared he must be. Then anger overwhelmed fear.

When I got to the rest stop, my confidence at being in a public place evaporated. According to the sign, the rest stop was closed for renovations as of the previous day. I could still enter as it wasn't blocked off yet, but the McDonald's was dark, and the only other vehicle in the lot was a huge bulldozer with an empty cab.

I pulled toward the back of the lot as the voice had instructed me. I wished I'd thought to grab at least a kitchen knife as protection. Not that I was even sure I'd have the nerve or dexterity to use it. There was a small picnic table under the shade of a maple tree. I shuddered as I remembered the last time I'd been here. After pacing around the table, not sure where I should be looking to see someone approaching, I finally sat down. I faced the lot where someone entering the rest stop would be visible, but I couldn't shake the cold, creepy feeling crawling up the back of my neck. I turned periodically to glance behind me at the small grassy strip and brush. A soft rustling in the underbrush made me yelp and jump up. I saw the fluffy white tail of a rabbit disappear through the weeds. I took several deep breaths and shook the tension out of my hands and shoulders, trying to calm my breathing and heart rate.

The time seemed to stretch forever as I waited for the person who had contacted me to arrive. My mind jumped from thought to thought. Why weren't they here already? Did they think I wouldn't show up? Maybe the flash drive wasn't what they wanted, maybe they had already hurt Bruno looking for—whatever. I squashed those thoughts quickly and tried to think things through. Someone wanted something that they thought I had and had taken Bruno to ensure I would give it to them. But in truth, there was no proof that they were the ones who killed Artie. As a matter of fact, the police seemed to think Rachel had murdered Artie, and while I didn't picture her as a killer, they must have some reason to charge her. But whoever they were, they were ruthless enough to take Bruno hostage to get what they wanted. Now I wished I'd taken the time to finish viewing what was on the flash drive I was about to give them. But if they wanted it, they were welcome to it, no matter what information it contained. My only concern was that they give me Bruno back safely.

Just as my courage built, I heard a car approaching the parking lot. I stood up, then sat again as I felt something poke me in the back and a voice say "sit."

"I have what you want! Where is Bruno?" A strong hand gripped the back of my neck, so I couldn't turn around. It felt like a vice and was shoving my head down until my face was squashed against the tabletop.

"Keep your head down and shut up."

I was sure I heard a car door slam now. A hoarse voice behind me said, "Bitch! I said no one else!" I felt a hard crack to the back of my head and my vision went fuzzy.

When my vision cleared, I was on my back by the picnic table, looking up at Justin McKenzie.

"Melanie! Are you all right?" He grabbed me by the arms and stabilized me as I struggled to a sit. "No, don't stand. You'll pass out."

My head felt like it was expanding then contracting rapidly. I started to shake it to clear my thoughts but stopped as this resulted in blinding pain. "Bruno! Where is he?" I looked around, careful to turn my head slowly.

"I don't know. He's not here." Justin said uncertainly. "I wasn't sure where you were at first. By the time I looked this way, I just saw you lying on the ground. There was some motion in the bushes behind you, but I couldn't see who or what it was."

I fought back the panic that my chance to get Bruno back may have just been thwarted. "Someone hit me. I think he saw you and ran. I told you not to come here."

"Well, it's a good thing I did. I'm sorry, but I didn't like the idea of you coming alone."

I ignored the fact that Justin was probably right. "They were pretty specific about what would happen if I wasn't alone. I wasn't willing to take a chance on them hurting Bruno."

"So instead..."

I shot Justin a look. His reply tapered off into a throat clearing.

I felt the back of my head as I got to my feet. There was a large knot forming, and my fingers came away with a smear of blood on them, but I didn't think I had a laceration big enough to need suturing. "I never saw Bruno; I don't think they brought him." That thought, more than the rap on the back of the head, was making me nauseous. I prayed he was all right.

"They never got what they came for either, though." I took the flash drive out of my pocket. I realized then that my purse, which I'd set on the seat next to me, was gone. "Whoever it was must have thought I'd put this in my purse." I held up the flash drive.

"What is it?"

"I didn't have time to look at the whole thing, but from what I saw, it looks like a series of numbers. I think maybe it was some sort of record of financial transactions. Maybe Artie owed someone money, and that's what they are after. I don't care. They can have it as long as they give Bruno back." I started to teeter toward the brush behind me.

"Where do you think you're going?" Justin grabbed my arm as I pitched unsteadily toward the right.

"I want to see how far this brushy area extends. They had to come from behind somehow."

"Never mind that, we should call the police. Let them explore where that area leads. I think you need to go to the Emergency Department and get your head checked out. You could have a concussion."

"No. No police. They were very clear that they would hurt Bruno if I involved the cops. And I'm fine. Really." He was most likely right about the concussion. There was a buzzing in my head like an entire hive of bees. I caught sight of something white a bit further in the bushes. A tissue. Next to it, my car keys. I bent carefully to pick each item up, seeing little floating lights each time I bent over. My wallet lay open, and everything was pulled out of it, but all that it contained seemed to still be there, even the nine dollars in cash I had in it. The contents of my purse were strewn like a trail of breadcrumbs until I found the purse itself. Justin helped me gather my things.

"So, you think it was the flash drive they want?"

"I'm pretty sure. I hope so because I can't bear to think of what else they would be after." I didn't mention the shadow he'd seen on Bruno's x-ray, but I saw the thought reflected in his face as he came to the same conclusion.

"You don't think—"

"I don't know. I hope whatever Artie did to Bruno has nothing to do with what they are after. Right now, I need to focus on getting him back." I bent to pluck more of my belongings from the underbrush.

I checked my cell phone, the screen was cracked from where it had landed on a rock, but it still worked. No messages from whoever took Bruno.

Justin took my arm gently and began to guide me back toward the parking area. "I don't want to sound like a broken record, but you need to see someone about your head, or at least to rest."

I didn't fight him. I figured the only thing I could do was to go home and pray Bruno's captors would contact me soon. As we emerged from the underbrush, I looked up to see a black pickup truck slow down as it drove through the rest stop, then suddenly accelerate. I yelled, "Hey!" and started to run unsteadily toward the truck.

"Did you see that?" I turned toward Justin.

"Could they have turned into the rest stop by mistake?"

"There's a big sign to say this stop is closed. What if it was someone checking to see if I was still here, and alone?" This last bit made me panic. Much as it was probably a good thing Justin showed up, what if his being here prevented the dog nappers from making contact again?

"All the more reason to get out of here. Let me at least drive you home; you still look a bit wobbly. You can pick up your car later."

"No. I'm fine to drive the short distance home." My reply came out a little bit more sharply than I'd intended. I reached up to feel the lump on the back of my head again. "I've been told by more than one person that I'm very hardheaded." I tried to give him my most reassuring smile, which wasn't easy, because inside I was shaking. I thought I'd seen a little furry head bouncing up and down in the passenger side window of the truck.

Chapter Twenty-Two

He tried to hang back, so I wouldn't notice him, but Justin followed me until I turned into the road that led to my house. I appreciated his concern, but I had begun to feel angrier and angrier about him showing up at the rest stop. True he'd saved me from what could have been more serious harm at the hands of whoever it was who had Bruno, but he also most likely scared them off before I could get Bruno back. I was about to pull over and tell him to stop following me, that I was fine and didn't need an escort home. However, he continued straight as I turned. Well, good. I had to believe that if I cooperated with them, Bruno's captors would keep him safe. I had to. I didn't know what else to do right now but sit and wait for them to contact me again. I prayed they would.

When I walked into the house, I could see that Lynn was home and had made dinner. Normally the fragrance filling the air would have my mouth watering, but I knew I'd never be able to swallow one bite of whatever it was in the covered dish on the stove. Lynn was at the sink, her back toward me.

"Holy Cow! You should have seen the drama at the office today. That Detective Cody came with two other officers and asked to speak with Rachel Harwood. They took her to the office down the hall, but I could hear her yelling about something and then crying. Next thing I knew they were escorting her out in handcuffs." She turned around and dropped the spoon she had been washing. "What happened? You have blood on the shoulder of your shirt! And you look white as a sheet. Here sit down." She pulled out a chair and gestured toward it.

I sat but waved away her hands as she reached to examine my head. "No.

It's ok. I'll wash it out, and it should be fine." I needed a few minutes to compose myself. "First, tell me what happened at the office. They really think Rachel killed Artie?"

"Well, as I said, they arrested her. They must have some strong evidence to suggest it."

I felt a jolt of emotional and mental overload. First Bruno was taken, now the apparent confirmation that Artie was killed by a friend and business partner. "What I don't get is why Rachel would kill Artie."

Lynn shook her head, "I don't know. She looked a mess, though when the police led her out of the office. She could barely walk. It looked like they were supporting her. Dr. Wang was trying to reassure her that it would be all right. He gave me the name of her attorney and told me to get him on the phone."

"I really didn't believe it was her. I thought she and Artie got along okay, and she seemed so overwhelmed by his murder," I said.

"I overheard Bobby telling Malcolm that the police found out that she and Artie had had a huge blow out fight shortly before he was murdered. I couldn't hear all of it, but something about how she blamed him for something to do with her sister. Then they shut the door to Malcolm's office, and I couldn't hear the rest of what was said. I'll nose around tomorrow and see if anyone's heard anything more." Lynn shut off the burner and poured the onion and mushroom mix over browned chicken she had arranged in a casserole dish. She turned to look around the kitchen a moment. "Where's Bruno? All tired out from his trip to 'Auntie Tori's'?"

"He's still missing." I fought against the lump rising in my throat. "I went to Tori's, but he wasn't there." I told her about finding Tori unconscious, the phone call from the captors, the flash drive in the pen and the aborted exchange attempt.

Lynn came to sit across the table from me, a stunned look on her face. "I thought my day was exciting." She jumped up and shut off the oven, covered the chicken, and put it in the refrigerator. "We have to do something. We should try to find him."

"Find him where? I have no idea where to start looking, or I'd already be there!" I took a deep breath. "I think we need to wait until they call back with directions on what to do next." I set my cell phone on the table, and we both stared at it as if it was a bomb. I willed it to ring, but nothing.

Lynn broke the silence. "What could Artie have done that involved Rachel's sister that would make Rachel angry enough to kill him?"

"Had an affair with her, got her pregnant? That would be pretty bad, but would it make Rachel want to kill him?" The truth was I was too upset over Bruno to do much thinking about anything else. "I am puzzled about something, though. If Rachel did kill Artie, and she's been arrested, who has Bruno? And are the two things even connected?"

Lynn just shook her head.

I stared at the phone, still no ring. I flashed on the black truck that had driven through the rest stop parking lot. I'd seen what looked like Bruno in the truck but did not see who was driving. I wasn't even sure if it was a man or a woman.

"What was on the flash drive you found?" Lynn said.

"I didn't get a chance to view all of it. From what I saw, it just looked like a bunch of numbers. Money amounts, I thought, but if so, it tallied up to a huge amount." I took the flash drive out of my pocket. "Now might be a good time to see if there is anything else on it that could help get Bruno back, or at least understand why it might be valuable to them."

I got my laptop and set it up on the table, and Lynn and I sat side by side, waiting for the flash drive to open. At first, all I saw was the same list of numbers and dates, but then I noticed that there was a small icon in the upper right-hand corner of the screen. I clicked on it, and a video came up. Even though the large "play" arrow was partially obscuring him, I could see the figure in the video was Artie. When the video started, he was sitting behind his desk at High Life Dermatology. He smiled and looked right into the camera. A lump rose in my throat, and I could hear Lynn gasp next to me.

"If you're watching this, it must be because I'm not around to collect the 'eggs' from the Golden Goose." He chuckled at his own joke, typical Artie, then started again. "Melanie, I hope it is you who finds this video. That was my intention, anyway. If my plan had succeeded, there would be no record of my take on the little venture I was involved in, nor would I be anywhere I could be found. If you found this, I must be dead. In that case, all I have stowed away is yours. The rest—the house, the cars, my official bank account, all my property—except for Bruno—will go to Tori. That will be in my will anyway. The money from the Golden Goose, which I will only ever mention here, is for you." He paused for a beat. "Oh, I have one request, however. Please send one million dollars to a woman named Lynn Duncan. I won't explain why here, but when you find her, you will know why I am asking you to do this."

He leaned back in his chair. He always loved drama. "I want to make amends for how our marriage ended. After the divorce, you always treated me civilly, even though you had plenty of reason not to. To get the money, go to the one who is always loyal to you. The one who I know was always deserving of your love. The information on how to get the money is there. Of course, I hope you never need to see this, that I am off spending the money myself." He shook his head and continued. "Anyway, I'm sorry for all the pain I caused you. You know I never stopped caring about you. I hope this helps a little." He blew a kiss.

I wiped a tear from my cheek. I couldn't look at Lynn yet, but I could hear her snuffling beside me.

Lynn got up to grab a couple of tissues off the counter and handed one to me. "That was so weird to see and hear Artie, as if he were alive again."

I blotted my cheeks. "I know. But in the end, he was just as arrogant and selfish as always. If he lived, we got nothing. I would have not even have seen his apology."

She gave a sharp laugh. "True."

Another thought struck me. "What's going to happen when Cody sees this? Now it looks like *I* have a motive to want Artie dead."

"One million dollars is no small amount either. What if the police think I was in it with you?"

We both just stared at the computer screen for a second. Artie's form frozen, blowing a final kiss.

"We're not keeping the money if we find it, are we?" Lynn said.

"Of course not. It was illegally gotten."

Lynn sighed. "Why couldn't he just leave us a small sum in his will like any normal person?"

I pulled the flash drive from the port on the computer. "It's Bruno. The one who is most loyal to me, the one who is most deserving of my love." My eyes began to tear up again, but for a different reason than before. "Justin saw an unexplained shadow on Bruno's x-ray. It must be some kind of hardware that explains where the money is. The money must be what the dognappers are after. Only I don't think they know where it is. I have to get him back before they figure out they have the key to the money's whereabouts in their hands already." I fought a mounting panic.

My cell phone finally made the ascending tones that were my ring tones. I nearly dropped the phone in my haste to answer it.

"You want the damn dog alive don't screw around with us this time. 10:30 at 1871 Chickadee Lane. Alone this time. No boyfriend, no cops. We will be watching. You try anything, and this time it will be more than a bump on the head." The voice was distorted again, but I knew who lived at that address.

The address they gave me was Artie's house. "Wait. Is Bruno with you? Is he all right? What about Tori? Why…?" They broke the connection.

"Well?' Lynn said.

"They want me to meet them at Artie's old address."

Lynn got up from the kitchen table as I did. "Why would they take Bruno back there? Is Tori still in the hospital? You don't think she's in on this, do you?"

"I don't know; she was in bad shape earlier today. I don't think they would have released her from the hospital yet. I don't know why there of all places, either." I grabbed my purse, being sure to tuck the flash drive back into my shorts pocket. "If Tori is in the hospital, the only other person I can think of who has access to the house is Zeta. She looks a lot like Tori, and I think she is the woman the receptionist at the Vet's office described as picking up Bruno." That was not good news since Bruno had not re-acted well to Zeta in the past, and I was worried what she would do to him if he didn't behave himself.

Lynn grabbed her purse. "Okay. What's the plan?"

"No! You can't come with me. They said alone. When Justin showed up at the rest stop they took off. I can't risk them leaving again if I show up with someone else." Or this time doing something worse to Bruno, I thought but didn't say.

"Come on, Melanie. You can't really be thinking of going alone. You just got through telling me what happened when you went to meet them alone earlier. It was a good thing Justin did follow you."

I had to admit that she was right.

"On top of which, it's pretty brazen of them to pick a place that you could use to tie in Zeta later. I'm going." She headed toward the door.

Everything she had said was right, and I felt relieved that she'd insisted. "Okay. But it has to look like I'm by myself. We need to go in two cars. The driveway is long. The house set back from the road. I want you to wait at the side of the road right before the driveway. There is a tall hedge along the road there. I don't think your car will be visible to whoever is in the house. I'll signal you when to pull over. If I don't come back out of the house in 15 minutes, call the police."

I patted the right-side pocket of my shorts to reassure myself I had the flash drive.

"Are you going to give them that? What if...?

"I know. But we don't have time to come up with anything else. I have to get Bruno and get out of there quick before they view the video. Or at least before they figure it out."

Chapter Twenty-Three

I felt a sinking feeling the entire way to meet Bruno's captors. How would it work, this exchange of a flash drive for Bruno? What if they had already figured out what I had to trade wasn't what they really wanted? I had to make them believe the location of the money was on the flash drive. My plan was to grab Bruno and leave before they viewed it. If they viewed the video first both Bruno and I would be in trouble, as I was sure they would want to know who it was who was so loyal to me. My experience had proved they weren't polite about asking for information.

The gorgeous, secluded area of North Madison where Artie had built his "castle" just seemed creepy now. The moon was only a slice in the sky, and there were no lights visible from any of his neighbor's houses, distant as they were. It was so dark I slowed three times thinking I was approaching the driveway before I found the actual entrance. I pulled over to the side of the road, and Lynn pulled behind me. As I got out to speak to her, she rolled down the window, and I whispered, "Fifteen minutes."

She nodded, "I got it." She grabbed my hand as I turned to walk back to my car. "I've been thinking. I don't know that this is such a good idea. Maybe we should call the police right now and wait for them to come before you go up to the house."

I considered it for a second, but then the thought of them harming Bruno made me decide to go as planned. "No. Wait just fifteen minutes, ok?" I strode back to my car, easing the door closed in case they were listening for me. I drove up the drive and parked in front of the garage.

I checked for other cars as I had on my previous visit to "Krapaneck Manor," but once again, there were none visible. It looked as if there was only a light on in one room on the first floor. As I walked through the portico toward the front door, I realized that I hadn't seen Elaina, Tori's housekeeper, on my last visit. She seemed very competent, poor woman. I hoped she'd at least gotten a good severance pay. I wiped my sweaty hand on my shorts, patting my pocket again to be sure it still contained the flash drive. I rang the bell and waited for someone to come. Several seconds passed, and no one had come to the door. I felt a chill down the back of my neck and turned around. I didn't see anyone. On impulse, I decided it might be better, and buy more time if I didn't have the flash drive on my person. I looked to see if there was a CCTV camera visible and, seeing none, jammed the pen with the flash drive under some ornamental rocks at the base of the shrubbery. I was getting more nervous now. Was anyone here? I tried the knob of the front door. Unlike the day I found Tori unconscious, this time, it was locked. However, as I took my hand away, the door was pulled open. The entranceway was dimly lit by light from the room adjacent to it. Whoever it was who opened the door must have stepped behind it, because I saw no one. Suddenly it didn't matter, because I heard Bruno barking and whining. He was really here this time, and he knew I was too. I rushed in without thinking or questioning.

What little light there was quickly became dimmer still. A cloth bag of some sort was thrust over my head, and someone grabbed my arms and yanked them behind me. I heard mumbling but couldn't make out the words. There was more than one of them, then. A voice that sounded like a munchkin on helium said, "Over here. Sit."

I nearly toppled over as I was shoved into a low chair with a padded seat and no arms. I heard what sounded like tape ripping, and my hands were bound behind me. I no longer heard Bruno barking. I made a split-second decision not to let on that I suspected Zeta was one of my captors.

"Where's Bru..." I got a hard rap on the head as soon as I began to speak.

"Stop that!" It was the munchkin voice again. I didn't know if they were talking to me or the person who'd hit me. In any case, I decided to hold my questions for a while until I got a better idea of what they were going to do.

CHAPTER TWENTY-THREE

The sack over my head was smooth textured and had a strong smell of Downy Field Fresh, so I thought it must be a pillowcase. Something about the munchkin voice the person was speaking in was familiar; then I remembered a visit I'd made to Mrs. Grant to check her blood pressure. Her grandson had a little red toy voice changer that he'd tormented us both with until the batteries died. I could feel the presence of someone standing in front of me.

"Where is the file with the information?"

My heart was pounding. I tried to estimate how long it had been since I arrived at the base of the driveway. Eight minutes, ten? I had to drag this out as long as I could so Lynn would know to call the police. "I have it. But how do I know you'll give me back Bruno safe and sound if I give you what you want?"

"Wouldn't you say we're the ones making the rules right now?" That voice was annoying.

"I just want to be sure of one thing. If I give you the file, then Bruno and I can just leave?"

There was a pause of several seconds during which I heard a whispering voice. It was definitely male, but not one I could identify. I could make out the words "not in purse" and felt something dropped at my feet.

"Stand up!" Squeaky voice again.

Before I could stand a pair of rough hands yanked me to my feet. He, I was sure it was a man, patted me from my shoulders on down and ran his hands up and down my legs, then pinched my backside. I tried to squirm away, "Stop it! You pig, cut that out."

The man chuckled and shoved me back into the chair. More whispering, and I thought I heard the word "car." I felt a draft as the door opened and closed. My relief at having hid the flash drive under the rocks evaporated. Then I had a more disturbing thought. I hoped I was right at how well the hedge at the start of the driveway blocked the view of the road. I heard my ringtone and felt a vibration against the side of my foot. My phone. I had forgotten to silence it before I got to the house. I had a brief hope that I could somehow hit the accept button, but before I could formulate a plan I felt the purse kicked away.

The voice changed. It was crackling and raspy now. "You better have brought that file with you! No more questions, no more games. Where is it?"

It had to have been fifteen minutes by now. Lynn should be calling the police any second, but I realized I still had to factor in how long it would take them to get here. I had no idea where in the house my captors were holding Bruno either. "First I want to know Bruno is here and that he is okay."

I felt a draft as the door opened and closed again. Something else was tossed at my feet, a cloth bag that fell with a clunk. Another purse?

Raspy voice again, "And I said to come alone. I'm afraid I had to disable your friend. Now give me the file."

I heard the male voice say in an angry whisper, "bitch—not much time." Then I felt a harder rap to the head, from behind this time. I briefly saw stars, followed by a flash of anger. "If you knock me out you'll never get the file." I felt sick to my stomach and it had nothing to do with head trauma, I was on my own. The police weren't coming and what the hell had they done to Lynn? "Show me Bruno is all right, and I'll tell you where to find the file."

I heard a sigh, no distortion now, then the squeaky voice again. "Get the dog but keep it away from her."

My plan was to get my hands free, grab Bruno, yell the location of the flash drive and get out of there. Unfortunately, I hadn't figured how all that was going to happen yet. As I waited for them to get Bruno, I said a silent prayer that Lynn was all right, and somewhere I could find her.

Finally, I heard Bruno's yip of welcome, and a whining and scrabble of his nails on a wooden floor. I was sure he was trying to reach me.

"Bruno! It's okay, boy. It's okay." I felt tears well up in my eyes.

Bruno let out a growl and two angry barks.

"Shit! Damn it! He bit me." The man's voice was undisguised now and one I'd heard someplace before.

"Take him back into the other room." There was another growl then a "yelp" and quiet.

I struggled to get up. "Let me loose. Undo my hands, and I'll get you the damn flash drive."

"What flash drive?" She didn't get the voice changer up fast enough. A woman's voice, throaty, no distortion. Zeta. And the man was the guy from the rest stop.

"Un-tape my hands, and you might as well take off the hood. I know it's you, Zeta. The information you want is on a flash drive. Artie hid it in one of his pens."

She made no move to remove the pillowcase from my head. "Hand it over." She sounded nervous now. "How do you know it contains the information we want? Have you looked at it?"

I concentrated on making my voice sound slightly annoyed. "No. You never gave me time after I found it." I hoped this was the right lie to tell. "I found a note in his papers that said to look for something valuable in his desk. I found a gold pen. It looked like the only thing that fit the bill."

I could hear heavy breathing as her companion came back into the room. "The little rat is back in his cage." He seemed to be talking to Zeta. "He up to date on his shots?" I assumed this was meant for me.

"Yes, but you could still get a wicked infection from a dog bite." I added under my breath, *"I hope!"*

"She says he put the information on a flash drive."

"Flash drive? You said it was on a microchip he hid somewhere." I heard a loud noise as if he had thrown something. "Nothing! Nothing about this whole thing has gone as planned! What the hell, Z?"

It sounded as if they were headed toward another part of the house, but it was still easy enough to hear most of what they were arguing about.

"Are you kidding me? You're the one who screwed it up. Nobody was supposed to get hurt!" All façade of calm was gone from Zeta. The term screaming banshee came to my mind.

"Did you want the bastard to run away with the fortune he'd skimmed from the operation? The women were just collateral damage."

"He was my brother-in-law! Do you know what it was like to try to keep who was responsible for his death from my sister? And you almost killed her too! Don't talk to me about plans not going well."

"Shut up! You're the one with the pocket full of painkillers. That was your own little bright solution! So there's plenty of blame to go around. Now we have even more problems." I knew he meant me.

I tried to pretend I hadn't heard the last exchange. I truly wished I hadn't because it didn't bode well for them keeping their promise to let us go. Although, it finally cleared up a few things. I cleared my throat and shouted, "If you untie my hands, I'll get the flash drive for you. I don't care why you want it. I'll just get out of here with Bruno."

I could hear the rapid approach of footsteps again.

I felt a swoosh of motion, and a firm hand grabbed the back of my neck and shook me like an old sock. "Where is it?"

"The pen is under some rocks lining the walk, near some shrubs. The flash drive is in the pen." I began to see flashes of light from the pressure on the back of my neck.

Zeta's voice, "I'll get it. You put her somewhere until we figure out what to do with her."

I was yanked to my feet again and shoved to my right for several feet, and then pushed around a corner. I struggled to break away, but he wrenched my arms up so high I thought my shoulder would be dislocated. "Look, the deal was I give you the information, you give me my dog back." My voice shook, in spite of my efforts to control it.

He snorted. "Well, plans change, don't they?"

I heard a door open, and my captor started to drag me down a flight of stairs. I tried to pull back, but stumbled and fell, careening off the last five or six steps. I attempted to turn and hunch my shoulders to keep my head from bouncing off the stairs but was only partially successful. I landed in a heap, my hands still behind me, my right shoulder throbbing, and my ears ringing. The only positive aspect of the fall was that my hood fell off.

It was the guy I had seen talking to Zeta at the funeral. Tori had called him Karl, I thought. He was muscular, but in a sinewy way like a runner, or a bike rider. He was several inches taller than me, with light colored hair and dark cold eyes. There were three scars raking down his left cheek. As Mr. Duggan said, a dark alley kind of guy. He whipped me up onto my feet.

"I meant to warn you to watch your step." He chuckled and shoved me against a wall and kicked my feet from beneath me. "Have a seat."

Obviously, he no longer cared that I knew what he looked like. That only confirmed my worst fears. He walked over to a workbench, his back to me. I struggled to get to my feet again, but he was quick. He came back and kicked my feet from beneath me again, a roll of duct tape in his hand.

"You have what you want. Please, just give me my dog and let me get out of here."

He snorted again, "Yeah, right." He slapped a piece of tape over my mouth. Next, he went to work wrapping tape twice around my ankles. I tried a trick I'd learned in a self-defense class I'd taken a few years previously. If you turned your feet outward with heels together, you could later create some slack by touching your toes together. He didn't seem to notice what I was doing.

He stomped back up the stairs, and I heard him yell, "Well, did you find it?"

I couldn't hear Zeta's answer. There was movement at the top of the stairs, then the rattling of Bruno's carrier as it bounced down the steps. "Here's your damn dog."

Bruno yelped once as he came down the stairs, but he righted himself inside when he landed. He frantically scratched at the door in an effort to get out to me. The latch must have been damaged in the fall, and the door of the carrier sprang open. Bruno bounded over to me, licking my face and arms, his whole body wagging with joy.

I couldn't even reassure him I loved him and missed him too since my mouth was taped shut. I frantically rubbed the tape off by drawing up my legs and rubbing the corner of my mouth on my knees. "Good boy! I missed you too." I whispered.

Bruno dipped his front end down, rear end up in his usual asking for play position, and barked expectantly at me.

"Shh! Come here, lie down!" He immediately obeyed me. Possibly for the first time ever.

It was very quiet upstairs. I figured that Zeta and her companion must be viewing the flash drive. I thought again about Artie as he appeared in the brief video at the end and realized time was running short. I figured they wouldn't take too long to get the reference to my dog. We had to get out of the basement before they decided to come after the microchip embedded in Bruno.

I placed my toes together, and sure enough, the tape became slack. It did me little good, however, since my hands were bound behind me, and I couldn't peel off the tape on my ankles. I struggled to loosen the tape on my wrists, but my right shoulder throbbed and threw a knife of pain up my neck every time I moved it. I looked around the room for something to use to break my wrist bindings. I was able to roll over and get my knees under me. Bracing against the wall, I came to a wobbly upright position. A row of tools hung neatly on a pegboard over the workbench. If I knew Artie at all, they hadn't been taken down since they were originally hung there. A saw glistened at the end of the row, and I briefly considered knocking it down to free myself but shuddered to think of the collateral damage I would likely do with that edge if I didn't strike the tape on my wrists right. Instead, I hopped/shuffled over to the workbench and used the edge of a shiny new vice clamped to the end to start to tear through the duct tape restraining my wrists. My shoulder blazed as if on fire as I jerked the last of the tape free. I snatched the binding off my ankles just as I heard movement upstairs again.

I looked for another way out, other than the stairs Bruno and I both had just been thrown down. I had no idea where my captors were in relation to that basement door, and I didn't want to bet on my ability to slip by them. I saw a short flight of stairs leading to a bulkhead door. I grabbed Bruno and threw the slide bolt, and tried to shove the door open. It wouldn't budge. It must have been locked on the outside also. I could hear the thud of something heavy falling or being thrown, followed by an exclamation and what sounded like more arguing. I couldn't make out what was being said. My guess was they had figured out what the information on the flash drive meant. I frantically scanned the basement for another way out. There were several small narrow windows lining the wall at ground level. I raced to the nearest one and unlatched it. It was at my eye level, so I'd have to boost myself up or find something to stand on. It sounded like footsteps rapidly crossing the room upstairs. I shoved Bruno out and said, "Run, boy!" Just then, I heard someone yank open the basement door. There was no way I'd ever make it up and out the window before they got downstairs. I ran to the end of the workbench, grabbed the shiny new hammer from the pegboard, and scooched down to hide. I realized it would only serve to give me time to think of "what next? rather than any hope, I wouldn't be noticed for more than a moment or two.

It was Karl who came down the stairs. I ducked back down, afraid to breathe.

"What the hell?" He bent to pick up broken bits of duct tape from the floor.

"Come on, bring them back up here!" Zeta yelled from upstairs.

I sunk farther back against the wall but must have rattled the pegboard holding the tools. The saw, a shower of assorted screwdrivers and wrenches, along with the pegboard itself came down around me. Karl whipped a small gun from his pocket and pointed it in my direction.

Before Karl could answer Zeta, the sound of the doorbell came from upstairs. "Get up and shut up. You make a sound, and you won't make it out of this basement." His voice was low, and the look in his eyes told me he meant it. "Get over here against the wall." He motioned to the spot where he'd originally dumped me.

I started toward where he had pointed, hoping to hide the hammer I still held behind my thigh. No luck.

"Drop it!" He hissed. And took his eyes off me for a second to look around. "Where's the dog?"

"He's gone," I said. As soon as the words were out of my mouth, however, there was a whining and scratching at the small window I'd shoved Bruno out of. He had come back for me.

Karl turned quickly toward the sound and pointed his gun at the window where I could see Bruno's little face peeking in. I snatched the hammer back up from where I had dropped it and threw it as hard as I could. It hit Karl in the back of the head, and he stumbled forward. His gun went off as he fell, and I heard a splintering as the bullet a beam instead of the window glass breaking. I raced past Karl and had just reached the stairs, when the lights suddenly blinked out. I froze in place.

They came back on just as suddenly. "Hands up. Madison Police."

My legs nearly gave out with relief. "Help! I'm—"

"Hands up, I said!" I was shocked to see that the officer at the top of the stairs had his weapon pointed at me.

I obeyed. But turned my head slightly to see Karl scrambling up off the floor. There was a wrenching sound as the bulkhead door opened, and another officer started down the stairs from that direction.

"Police. Freeze." This officer had his gun trained on Karl, who was edging toward the gun he had dropped when he fell. "Leave it. Hands up."

I turned back toward the police officer at the top of the stairs. "Officer, my name is Melanie Bass, and I...."

"Keep your hands up, miss. Walk slowly up the stairs."

I did as I was instructed, never taking my eyes from his gun. "But, I..."

"Melanie! Officer, that's the woman I told you was missing." Justin had suddenly appeared behind the police. He was followed by another policeman who quickly grabbed his arm and pulled him away from the open doorway at the top of the stairs.

The first policeman lowered his weapon. "Sorry, miss, but until we got things straightened out, everyone was under suspicion."

I could hear a scuffle behind me. Karl evidently was not being as cooperative as I had been. My legs shook as I rushed up the remaining stairs toward Justin. I went to embrace him briefly, unsure of how he happened to get there, but instead found myself leaning on him as I began to shake uncontrollably. "Where's Lynn? And we need to get Bruno. He was trying to get back into the basement after me."

There was a background noise of crackling radios, and codes I couldn't understand, but the only sound I could focus on was the sound of happy barking and scuttle of feet as Bruno bounded up the stairs toward me, a female officer in hot pursuit. "Hey, come back here!"

I scooped him up and held him in a tight hug as he licked my face. "This is Bruno. This is my dog." I said to the officers.

"He dashed around me as we were securing the outer door again," the officer who had chased him said.

"What about Lynn? Is she all right?" I looked at the officer who had been holding me at gunpoint.

"Ms. Duncan suffered a few bumps and lacerations, we are having her taken to the emergency department to be checked out, but she was alert and talking when we found her. We'll need an official statement from both Ms. Duncan and you. But for now, she filled us in on what was going on here."

I heard Zeta's voice coming from another room. "When my attorney gets here, I will answer your questions, not before."

I didn't care how good her attorney was. She was going to have some explaining to do over how I came to be restrained in the basement of her sister's house.

Chapter Twenty-Four

The police allowed Justin to drive me to the station so they could take my statement. When we arrived at the police station I refused to let them separate me from Bruno again, but Justin said he would take care of him while I spoke to one of the officers. The last I saw of Karl he was being loaded into the back of a squad car, still writhing and swearing that he had done nothing wrong. Zeta was led to another car, looking as unconcerned as if she wore handcuffs every day.

I looked at Justin as we pulled behind the police cars. “So, how did you know where I was?”

He blushed. “It’s my grandfather’s fault. You know how he’s such a mystery buff, well he loves to listen to his police scanner. He got me interested and bought me one for Christmas. Geeky, huh?”

I laughed. “No, I am well acquainted with your grandfather’s monitoring of police activity. I’d say I’m pretty lucky you developed an interest too. But how did the cops know where to go? How did you?”

“I’m not sure who reported a problem, but there was quite a bit of chatter back and forth while they traced a 911 from a woman. Thanks to my grandfather, I learned a lot of the codes. From what I could make out, they had a hostage situation, and they gave the address. It sounded familiar. I deleted the phone number and address of your ex after what happened with Bruno, but I did remember some of the address before I got rid of it. I thought I would drive out here just in case you were involved.”

“Lynn! She got a chance to make the call after all!” I started to text Lynn to check on her but realized she may not have her phone on her any longer.

"Can we go to the hospital after we are finished at the police station? I want to check on Lynn."

I told the officer who took my statement everything that had happened that day, starting with the attack at the rest stop. I told him I had heard Zeta accuse Karl of killing Artie and the two women, and that he didn't deny it. I also explained what was apparently the motive for Artie's murder. "The flash drive I found is probably still in Zeta's computer."

"No, it was retrieved and is being held as evidence. I'm sure one of the detectives will want to talk to you about your interpretation of the information it contains."

I nodded.

The door opened, and I heard a familiar voice. "Hello again, Miss Bass. I'm sorry it took me so long to get your message and return the call. From what I heard, you had a very busy evening yourself."

Sunny Cody certainly had a very dry sense of humor. Also, a tendency to understate things quite a bit. "Was that your call I missed while Zeta and Karl were holding me hostage?" I thought back to the vibrating phone in my purse.

She sighed as she settled into a chair. "Yes, I did try to call you back. You sounded so distraught in your message I was concerned when you didn't answer. I called the department to see if they'd received any distress calls involving you. When they sorted out the mystery 911 call, they notified me."

She seemed to have been brought pretty much up to speed already, and I filled in the details she didn't have. Actually, I think I blathered on a bit more than she even needed, but I couldn't seem to stop retelling the whole story as if to reassure myself it really happened and that Lynn, Bruno, and I all were all right.

"So back to your earlier phone call to me. Did you suspect then that Zeta Hauser and Karl Duchaine were involved in the deaths of your husband and Jeanine Sykes? Is that the information you referred to?"

I shook my head. "No. It was that I found the flash drive, and that some kind of information is on a microchip embedded in my dog Bruno." I had been vague about what was on the flash drive in my report, but felt I had to come clean with Cody. "Apparently, there is a large amount of money involved. I think that is what Zeta and Karl were after. I'm all but certain the money he referred to was related to Kerabolt, the drug he was using illegally. He called it the Golden Goose."

She had her pad and pen out and was scribbling a few notes as I spoke. "Where is your dog now? Has the micro-chip been recovered yet?"

I felt a small lump of ice start to form in my stomach. "My friend is watching Bruno. No. The chip is still there as far as I know." I couldn't bear to think of poor Bruno having to undergo another trauma.

"I'm sorry, but we will have to impound the dog until we recover the microchip." She sounded sympathetic.

"No! You can't take him away from me again! Couldn't we recover the chip tonight? My friend is also Bruno's vet. He could remove it tonight. Please." I was sure Justin would do it if I asked. Or, at least pretty sure. He did come looking for me after all.

She hesitated. "Someone from the department would have to be present. There is a chain of evidence to maintain."

The panic I felt must have shown on my face as I came out of the interview room. Justin jumped up from the chair he had been waiting in. "Is everything all right? What happened?"

I fought to control my voice. "Detective Cody said they have to keep Bruno until they recover the microchip from him." I bent to scoop Bruno into my arms, and he licked my face. "I don't want to be separated from him again. Do you think you could do that? Tonight? Please?"

He paused for a few minutes before answering, and I was afraid he was going to say he couldn't do it. "Yes, of course. We could do it right in the office. You could assist me."

Detective Cody had followed me out of the interview room, and he looked to her for confirmation.

She looked hesitant, but then nodded.

He smiled and said, "The whole procedure shouldn't take more than twenty minutes start to finish. I'll use a local anesthetic, so you can take Bruno home afterward. That won't be a problem, will it, Detective?"

"Thank you!" I squashed Bruno between us a little as I gave Justin a hug with my free arm.

Justin had Bruno, Detective Cody, and me wait in the waiting room at the veterinary office as he went in back to the procedure room to set up for the microchip removal. Bruno curled up in my lap as I settled onto one of the padded benches. Detective Cody paced the room, reading the labels on the prescription dog food displayed, and picking up and putting down pamphlets on puppy care, flea prevention, and the benefits of neutering your pet. Just as she turned to show me a framed photo of the Pet Preventative Pet of the week, an Australian Shepard who looked surprised and embarrassed at the honor, Justin came to get us.

I stood calming Bruno as Justin worked to remove the chip. True to his word, he used lidocaine to numb the area around where the chip seemed to be located. Bruno never even flinched when Justin made the small incision. I handed him some gauze squares to mop up the small trickle of blood that followed the track of the scalpel and held a retractor as he probed for the microchip. I turned around when I heard a soft gagging sound and the "whoof!" of someone sitting down hard.

"Are you all right?" I said. Detective Cody was the color of raw pizza dough.

"Fine." She wiped a hand across her face. "A little dehydrated is all." She slowly got back up, but I noticed she stayed a bit farther back from the procedure table.

I hid a smile as I turned back to Bruno.

Justin used a forceps to extract the micro-chip, which looked even smaller than I had imagined. "Here you are, Detective." He dropped it into an evidence bag she held out.

Detective Cody hurried from the room, and I stayed to hold Bruno as Justin put in a couple of sutures to close the small wound.

I asked the detective before she left, "Would it be possible to let me know what the chip contains? I mean, I know I can't keep the money, and I don't want it. But after the way it disrupted my life, I'd like to know how much he planned to take off with, and where it was hidden."

She nodded. "I'll let you know what I can."

Bruno lay totally relaxed in my arms as we left the office. It was as if he knew the whole bad episode was finally over. I called the Emergency Department at the hospital and learned that Lynn had been released and was going home, so decided to meet her there.

Justin offered to drive me home, but I really wanted to retrieve my car from Tori's. I suddenly realized that I finally did think of it as Tori's house, not Artie's any longer.

"Thanks, but what I would like, if you don't mind driving me, is to go to pick up my car. I'd rather get it over with, so I have no reason to go back to that house again after tonight."

"All right, but only if you'll allow me to follow you back to your house afterward."

I didn't even attempt to argue this time.

When we reached my driveway, I got out of my car to thank him again for his help. "You must be exhausted, but would you like to come in for some coffee or tea? I want to hear what Lynn has to say about what happened to her, and I'm too keyed up to sleep right now."

"Are you kidding! I was trying the entire way here to think of a polite way to invite myself in." Even though it was dark, I thought I saw him blush. "I mean, I don't think I can sleep yet either, and I want to hear what your friend has to say, too."

Bruno wagged all over as we entered the house from the side door, seeming to have no aftereffects at all from his procedure.

Lynn had her back to us, having set her easel up on a drop cloth in the kitchen. There was a canvas propped on it, covered with blobs and swirls of black, purple, and green. Lynn herself was also covered with splotches and swirls. Some of them, I realized, were not paint but bruises. She whirled around as we entered, her brush clutched to her middle like a knife. "Oh! You're home!" She started to rush toward me, her arms out to embrace, but stopped and looked down at herself. "Sorry. I was getting a little inner Jackson Pollack out."

I grabbed her in a hug anyway. "Thank you. The police arrived just in time. Are you all right? What did he do to you?"

She wiped her hands on a rag and stooped to stroke Bruno and murmur to him, then gave Justin a questioning look.

He smiled and held out his hand. "Justin McKenzie."

"You remember me telling you about Justin? He's the new vet who has been helping Bruno," I said.

After they shook hands, Lynn looked from one to the other of us. "Is Bruno all right? It's late for any type of doctor to be making a house call."

"I'll explain later. It's a long story," I said. "We want to hear what happened to you."

I had Lynn settle into a chair, Bruno in her lap, and I put on the kettle for tea.

"I waited for fifteen minutes, like you said. It was a long fifteen minutes, I might add. I had just dialed 911 to tell them I thought my friend was in danger, when someone broke the driver's side window and yanked me by the hair, holding a gun to my head. I never even saw him approach the car." She stopped and swallowed. I could see her hands had started to shake a bit.

"I tried to yell, but he hit me with something, and I lost consciousness for a few seconds, I think. Next thing I knew, he was binding my hands and ankles with duct tape, and he had stuffed something into my mouth. The phone fell onto the floor of the car when he hit me. It must have landed halfway under the seat or something. In any case, I guess he didn't see it. I pretended to be unconscious until he left then I tried to talk around the gag, or at least make some kind of noise." She smiled sheepishly. "Lot of good my Krav Maga training did tonight. Guess I should have finished the course."

I reached out to rub her arm. "Are you kidding! Your quick thinking saved us."

I told her how the police were able to trace the call, Karl admitting to killing Artie, and Bruno's late-night surgery, and Justin's part in what happened.

It was very close to dawn when we finished going back over the evening's events, and Justin stretched and yawned. "I will let you ladies get some rest." He bent to pat Bruno and check the three stitches in his shoulder. "I can take these out in a week. If he has any problems before then, please let me know."

I got up as Justin started toward the door. "A week? I can take them out myself. But, I was hoping maybe you'd be able to stop over for a little dinner. Say tomorrow night?" I was too tired for subtlety. I gave him a quick kiss. "And thank you for everything you did tonight. And thank you for not listening when I told you not to follow me today."

He just grinned and said, "Tomorrow evening sounds great!"

Chapter Twenty-Five

The sun was about to come up by the time Justin left, but sleep was still not an option for me. I went to bed, Bruno closely snuggled by my side, but couldn't stop thinking of Artie's death and his having hid the microchip in Bruno. I was deeply disturbed by what he did. It meant I would have to hurt someone I loved, someone I thought he loved, to claim a financial gain. An ill begotten gain, too. I had never thought of Artie as a bad person. Self-centered, yes. Egotistical at times and certainly deceptive. But not uncaring. I had loved him once, his charm and intelligence outweighing what seemed then like minor flaws. I shifted positions in bed. Bruno sighed and shifted too as I stroked his neck, careful of the sutures closing the small wound. Most likely, Artie had never thought ahead to the consequences of what he had done. Another one of his flaws.

I was surprised to be awakened by a beam of light shining through the edge of the blinds on my bedroom window. That meant it must be early afternoon, and I had slept after all. Bruno was also awake, staring intently at me as if to make sure I was still there. I scratched his ears and gave him a kiss on the top of the head, then stretched and slipped out of bed. I padded out to the kitchen to find a note from Lynn on the kitchen table.

"Went in to work at noon. Fed and took Bruno out before I left. See you later. Lots to rehash! L."

I had left a message on the machine at my work as soon as we got home the night before explaining that I wasn't able to make it in. I had a light schedule today and was sure Judy would be able to cover me. I took Bruno out again, and after playing with him a bit, decided there was something else I needed to do. I would pay a visit to High Life Dermatology. There still was a lot unexplained around Artie's involvement with Kerabolt, and who knew what about what was going on.

The atmosphere in the High Life Dermatology office was subdued. Lynn was on the phone speaking softly when I walked in; she lifted one eyebrow but showed no other reaction. Half a dozen patients filled the chairs, magazines shielding their faces. One gentleman held the morning Register, the front-page headline about the investigation into unapproved medical treatments at High Life Dermatology discreetly folded over. I wondered how many of these people were the faithful, who just didn't believe their doctor could do wrong, and how many were mercilessly curious – eager to get the full scoop from Bobby or Malcolm on what had really happened.

Lynn's voice, firm and professional, cut through the silence. "Ms. Bass, I'll need you to fill out these forms, please."

I approached the reception desk where she pretended to be taking down some information from me. "Thanks. How are you doing?" I could still make out the bruise near her temple through the concealer she had used.

"I'm okay. Tired and a little achy. How about you?"

"The same. Is Bobby in today, I have a few questions for him."

Lynn whispered, "They're both swamped, he's still with a patient, but after that I can slip you in."

Just then, Malcolm exited one of the examination rooms. His eyes met mine, and he seemed to freeze in place for a moment. "Melanie. Can I have a word with you?" He waved me toward his office.

"Have a seat," he said, motioning toward the big leather chair facing his desk.

I couldn't help but notice the framed picture on the wall behind him of the four partners: Bobby, Malcolm, Artie, and Rachel. It had been taken several years before, when they first opened the practice. They were standing in front of the sign "High Life Dermatology." Malcolm had an arm around both Artie and Bobby.

Malcolm took a seat on the other side of the desk. He looked to be in better shape than I'd seen him in years. His eyes were clear, his dark hair newly barbered, his cologne subtle, not poured on to hide the scent of stale booze. His color was good, and he seemed focused. We stared at each other for a second or two.

"My god, Melanie! How are you? I can't believe what you just went through. Ms. Duncan told us what happened last night."

"I am way past the point of being polite, Malcolm. Did you know about how Artie was getting Kerabolt, that he was doing it illegally? That he apparently wasn't sharing the full profit with either the practice or his partners in crime?"

He took a moment before replying. "Look, I can't discuss the whole Kerabolt thing or my part in it. My lawyer's orders. I will say I had my suspicions about where the drug was coming from but was never sure exactly what was going on. I suspected Artie was still prescribing Kerabolt, even after warnings of potentially serious side effects were published. As far as the monies he was making from it, I never knew exactly how much it was or who he was involved with. That's all I can say."

"It must have been quite a bit of money. Didn't you or the others question where it was coming from?"

His color began to rise, but he looked right at me. "I'm not saying I'm not ashamed of ignoring it, but what he did brought a lot of new patients into the practice. I assume they had heard of the new miracle treatment Artie was offering. I can't speak for the others, but it was easy for me at the time to rationalize that the extra money was coming from an increased patient load, not that he was selling them a dangerous drug himself and charging them an outrageous price for it."

"What about Rachel? Do you think she knew Artie was prescribing Kerabolt?"

"That is what the argument between Rachel and Artie was about. He sold the 'miracle' of the drug to Rachel's sister, and the sister got colon cancer. Rachel blamed Artie for giving her the drug. I have never seen Rachel so angry. She threatened to turn Artie over to the authorities. It was Artie who pointed out to her the implications of what that would do to the practice in general. After that, things got pretty tense around here. I wonder if Rachel threatening him is what made Artie decide to run away."

I shook my head. "That's a possibility. But poor Rachel. I take it she didn't know about the possible side effects when she gave it to her sister."

He sighed, then said, "No, I don't think so."

"She must have been released after the real killer was identified." I felt a quick chill at the memory of Karl holding that gun on me, and then Bruno in that basement.

"Actually, she was released before you confronted Zeta and her partner. It's not a crime to be angry enough to kill someone, only if you carry through on it."

I thought, *Good thing, or Artie would have been dead long ago.* "Is Rachel on leave from the practice?"

Malcolm nodded. "Yeah. I think she blames herself too. For not investigating the drug further before she gave it to her sister. She took a leave to care for her."

"How about Bobby? He claims he had no part in using Kerabolt, and he had advised Artie against it."

"As far as I know, that's true. Like I said, I can't say much during the investigation."

"What's going to happen now? With the practice, I mean."

Malcolm shrugged. "It will do okay. I have to settle my own legal problems, and Rachel will be missed. But Bobby and Alex will carry it until I get the mess I'm in straightened out."

"Good. I know you have a lot of loyal patients." At least a half dozen or so, anyway.

He looked down at his desk, as if he couldn't meet my eyes. "It's what happened to Renata that hurts the worst. I think she knew some of what was going on with Artie and his cohorts. She was loyal to all of us, I think she was just trying to keep Artie and me out of trouble. I'm not sure how she was involved, but when the police showed me the fake research protocol I realized it was Renata's handwriting. She would have done anything he asked."

I cleared my throat, "I'm sorry about Renata. I'm not sure I ever told you that. I think she was trying to warn me before she was killed. I think maybe she knew who was after me. My roommate Lynn heard a scuffle in the background the night she called me, then she was killed the next day."

"That bastard should burn in hell for what he did to her." He looked as if he might be tearing up. "What a fiasco, huh? How is Bruno, by the way?"

"He's fine now. Still a little skittish at times, but I'm getting him help."

I stood up to leave, and Malcolm stood up also, and took my hand. "I'm sorry for everything, Melanie. I'm.... just sorry."

I patted the hand holding mine, "Good luck, Malcolm."

I stopped at the front desk to tell Lynn that I didn't need to see Bobby after all, my conversation with Malcolm was all I could handle for one day. I told her I'd catch up with Bobby Wang later. I noticed the shiny new sign on the door to the office directly to the side of the desk, Artie's old office. It said "Alex Drover M.D." A teenage girl with acne stood saying goodbye to a tall sandy haired man in glasses. As she left, Alex Drover flashed me a smile that could have come from a Crest commercial. I smiled back and nodded.

Lynn nudged me and whispered, "A hunk, what did I tell you? So, what do you think?"

He stood briefly framed in the doorway I'd passed through a thousand or more times in what seemed a lifetime ago. I thought about Justin and felt a quick burst of excitement at the thought of seeing him that night. "Me? Not a chance. But...." I nudged her.

Chapter Twenty-Six

Three days after the incident at Chickadee Lane, I got a call from the police.

"We have some of Dr. Krapaneck's belongings here. Detective Cody said you might want to come down and claim them. Just bring the receipt for the items with you when you come."

"But I thought Artie's widow, Tori, was supposed to receive the things the Detective removed from my house. I don't—"

He cleared his throat. "Mrs. Krapaneck is unavailable at this time. Detective Cody said maybe you would want them."

No, I did not want them. I had all I wanted of mementos in the form of the pillow I'd embroidered for him, and more than enough in memories, good and very bad. "Why don't I just leave them there for now. I'll contact one of his former partners and see if they need anything you may have."

"Sure, okay. Have them bring the receipt, though."

As I ended the call, Lynn came home, carrying her supplies from one of the evening art classes she taught. "You don't look very happy. That wasn't a call from Justin having to cancel plans, was it?"

I smiled, "No. We're still going out again on Saturday. That was the police department. They said I could pick up the things Detective Cody took after we cleaned out Artie's office. I'll call Bobby and see if he wants them. The officer said they couldn't drop them off at Tori's. She wasn't available. You didn't hear anything at the office about what is going on with her, did you?"

"No, nothing. But we've been so busy there hasn't been much time for gossip."

"As much as I'm not a fan of hers, I hope Tori is all right. She wasn't there the night everything happened, and I never found out where she was." I punched in Bobby Wang's number.

After I delivered the message about Artie's belongings, I said, "Has Tori gone away somewhere to recover from Artie's death? I think she was still in the hospital the night... everything happened. But now the police said they couldn't reach her."

"Oh, the police know where she is. They were just being mindful of her privacy. That lovely sister of hers and her cretin of a boyfriend got her hooked on pills. She's in rehab. A discrete place out of state."

"Oh, I'm sorry to hear that. I mean, I'm glad she is getting help. When I found her unconscious that day, she was pretty close to a lethal overdose."

"She's getting better, I hear. She'll be pleased to hear you asked about her."

I didn't know about that, but I did feel sorry for her.

Bobby cleared his throat. "I guess I owe you an apology. I never meant to get you involved in that mess when I asked you to pick up Artie's things at our office."

"It wasn't your fault. It was Artie's fault. Even his involvement with Kerabolt when he thought he might be helping someone was overlaid with pride and greed."

"That is true, but until he got involved in that, he was a great doctor, and I miss him as a friend."

We said our goodbyes, and I felt like there was a note of finality to it all.

I had convinced myself that it was safe at last to put Artie to rest, when Detective Cody showed up at my door the following day. She came in and sat in the chair I motioned towards.

"I said I would let you know what we found on the micro-chip we removed from your dog." She cleared her throat. "Your ex-husband must have been a very good businessman as well as a well-known physician. He had amassed more than 3.5 million dollars. According to Ms. Hauser, who by the way was very agreeable to co-operate with us once offered a deal, those funds were what he skimmed off the profits he kept separate from what he put into the practice."

"And Zeta and Karl were supposed to have shared in those profits?"

"That's what Ms. Hauser has alleged. According to her, Dr. Krapaneck had been only giving them a fraction of the money promised. He was preparing to leave the country and disappear, keeping the bulk of the money that he had transferred to an offshore account. Ms. Hauser said her sister had been dropping hints about him promising to take her on a long vacation, and this led to her suspicions."

So, what we suspected about Artie leaving his partners broke and holding the bag was true. "Has the FDA been able to trace the supply path back to Zeta?" If so, even if she was not charged with being involved in the murder, she would be in trouble on at least one other front.

Detective Cody paused a moment before answering. "I can't speak for another agency."

I took that as a "yes."

She got up as if to leave. "I'm only sharing the information I have because I promised you I would let you know what was on that microchip."

I had one more question. "Where was the money hidden?"

"What we found was the offshore bank account number where most of the money was deposited, but there also was $200,000 in large bills. The combination to the safe where he hid the money and account number was also on the chip." She smiled. "The safe was behind the tool pegboard in his basement."

The pegboard that had nearly hit me in the head. I wondered if Zeta and Karl knew how close they were to getting what they wanted, if they suspected the information they wanted was hidden somewhere in the house, and that was why they had me meet them there.

Detective Cody shook my hand before she left. "Good luck, Ms. Bass, and I hope we don't have any reason to see each other again. No offense meant, of course."

I smiled in return, "Oh, believe me, Detective, none taken."

Acknowledgements

Thank you to my writers group Roberta Isleib (Lucy Burdette) and Ang Pompano. Their suggestions, encouragement, and occasionally much needed 'nudges' and advice have helped immensely in the writing of this book. Most of all I would like to thank you for your friendship.

I would like to thank Laura and Josh Falcone for technical help whenever I needed to figure how to perform an unfamiliar task whether it be on my computer or on social media. I appreciate your patience with my ineptitude!

Thank you to my wonderful agent Cindy Bullard and the people at Level Best Books – the amazing editors Harriette Sackler, Shawn Reilly Simmons, and Verena Rose.

I appreciate the support and interest of my former nursing colleagues who knew of my efforts to write and get published. Also thank you for the many experiences we shared and stories we told. No material is wasted.

Finally, I must thank my family for their love and support over the years. Your understanding and encouragement have made all the difference. Thank you Rich, Laura, Josh, Jeffrey, Dan, Mary, Jason, and Rich Jr.

About the Author

Christine Falcone's short stories have appeared in publications such as *Imagine, Lancrom Review,* and *Deadfall: Crime Stories by New England Writers.* After working for nearly forty years as an RN in a Neonatal Intensive Care Unit, Christine is delighted that retirement coincides with the publication of her first full length mystery, *EX'd Out.*

She lives on the Connecticut Shoreline with her family and a dog who is not nearly as well behaved as Bruno, the beloved canine in her novel.

SOCIAL MEDIA HANDLE:
Christine Falcone (Facebook)

AUTHOR WEBSITE:
www.christinefalcone.com

CPSIA information can be obtained
at www.ICGtesting.com
Printed in the USA
BVHW041647181022
649734BV00005B/80

9 781685 121785